'Just because I left home doesn't mean I didn't think about you.' Jack immediately cursed himself. Why had he said that?

'Yeah, right.' Cleo glared at him, her mouth compressed to a grim line, at odds with the soft play of sunlight over her face. She crossed the room again, coffee obviously forgotten. 'I stopped thinking about *you* a long time ago. You're history, Jack. You may think you're God's gift to women, but not to *this* woman. This woman wants more than a quick roll between the sheets and a kiss goodbye.'

The thought of a naked Cleo in bed with some faceless man was a black hole he always took pains to steer clear of. 'I damn well hope so,' Jack replied.

When not teaching or writing, **Anne Oliver** loves nothing more than escaping into a book. She keeps a box of tissues handy—her favourite stories are intense, passionate, against-all-odds romances. Eight years ago she began creating her own characters in paranormal and time travel adventures, before turning to contemporary romance. Other interests include quilting, astronomy, all things Scottish, and eating anything she doesn't have to cook. Sharing her characters' journeys with readers all over the world is a privilege…and a dream come true. Anne lives in Adelaide, South Australia, and has two adult children.

This is Anne's debut book for Modern Extra!

BEHIND CLOSED DOORS...

BY
ANNE OLIVER

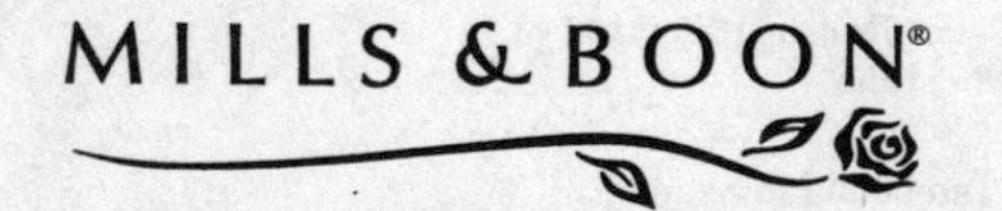

First published in Great Britain 2006
Harlequin Mills & Boon Limited,
Eton House, 18-24 Paradise Road, Richmond, Surrey TW9 1SR

ISBN-13: 978 0 263 84994 3
ISBN-10: 0 263 84994 5

Set in Times Roman 10½ on 12 pt.
171-0806-51363

Printed and bound in Spain
by Litografia Rosés S.A., Barcelona

BEHIND CLOSED DOORS...

Thanks

With thanks to my critique partners Kathy, Trish, Linda and Sharon who encouraged me to just *go for it*! Thank you also to my husband Henry and life-long friend Sue, both of whom believed in me, and to Kimberley Young for giving me this opportunity.

Dedication

In memory of my dad.

CHAPTER ONE

IT WASN'T the homecoming he'd pictured. Jack Devlin pushed his sunglasses higher on his nose and stared at the two-storey house he'd lived in for the first twenty-one years of his life. For the past six years he'd been pretty successful in making a point of *not* picturing it.

Perhaps that was the reason he was tripping through this emotional minefield now. Being dead didn't exonerate his father, but Jack had to concede he himself should have attempted some sort of reconciliation years ago.

But he wasn't the same naïve young man who'd left without a backward glance. The Jack Devlin who'd scaled that trellis to his room at three a.m. till he knew the steps blindfolded and backwards seemed like someone else.

And the woman he was about to come face to face with was no longer the sixteen-year-old kid he'd left behind.

He cursed the familiar gut-punch that always accompanied that particular image and hooked a finger inside the too-stiff collar of the shirt and black tie he'd picked up at Melbourne International Airport. In this suffocating summer heat he could almost feel those memories reaching out to strangle him.

She'd be here. No matter what she'd been up to since Jack had last seen her, Cleo Honeywell would not miss his father's funeral.

His jaw tensed as he reached for his bag. He frowned down at the shirt's packaging creases as he hefted the pack and winced as pain shot through his injured shoulder. So much for returning in style.

The heavy aroma of greasy food wafting through the open windows overlaid the outdoor's fragrance of lemon-scented gums. The resulting nausea churned in his stomach and the headache that had been building behind his right eye now throbbed in time with The Easybeats' 'She's so Fine' pumping from the stereo. No prizes for guessing who'd selected Dad's favourite musical entertainment—Cleo was obviously this afternoon's hostess.

The ground heaved and he slumped against one of the verandah pillars, gritted his teeth. Damn painkillers were wearing off. What he needed was sleep, twelve hours of blessed uninterrupted oblivion. But that wasn't likely to happen any time soon. With a deep breath, he slipped his glasses in his shirt pocket, pushed away and stepped inside.

He'd missed the funeral by a good two hours, but apparently the party wasn't over yet. A motley bunch of senior citizens in psychedelic seventies gear were still in full swing, Ben Hargreaves included. His father's solicitor was wearing a lime and purple tie and flares. A fancy dress funeral. And why the hell not? One corner of Jack's mouth lifted at an irony only he could appreciate. A fitting finale for the quintessential wolf in sheep's clothing.

Then his gaze snagged on the woman in the red and white daisy-splashed halter dress with a spectacular rear end as she slung her arms round Ben's neck for a slow dance. Her skirt—if you could call the scrap of fabric a skirt—hiked several inches to reveal equally spectacular thighs.

A different kind of heat stirred his lower body. There wasn't a whole lot of her, perhaps five-two if you discounted the platform shoes, but the curves were all there and in all the right places. His photographer's eye admired the form, but it was a purely masculine hum that slid through his veins.

Then she turned slightly and he got his first look at her profile.

Cleo.

For the second time in as many minutes the old punch slammed into his solar plexus. He set his pack down before he dropped the thing as what little strength he had left drained from his limbs.

He could try telling himself it was jetlag, or the fact that he'd discharged himself from hospital against the doctor's advice and grabbed the first flight out of Rome. *Face it, Devlin, you've never gotten Cleo out of your system.* Still those slumberous blue eyes, that wild-in-the-moonlight hair. For years he'd imagined how that hair would feel in his hands, how it would look on his pillow.

At sixteen she'd been off limits, a beauty with a chip on her shoulder you could carve a monument from. He didn't know about the attitude, but her looks had only improved.

She'd twisted her hair up into one of those clasp things that showed off her nape and made her look elegant and casual at the same time. Her full mouth, more often than not set in a pout, had been one of his forbidden fantasies.

She wasn't pouting now and her smile was as stunning as he remembered. But then, he thought with a wry grimace, she hadn't seen *him* yet.

His throat was suddenly parched. Right now he'd kill for a cold Aussie beer. Or something stronger to mask the feelings that had sprung to life again as if the past few years hadn't existed.

Watching her, he steeled himself against anger, resentment, regret, and, churning through it all, the burning sense of loss for this girl who'd grown into a woman.

All ancient history. He let out a slow, tired breath. The sooner he finalised his father's affairs, sold the house and got out of here, the better.

He was here.

Cleo knew by the way her scalp tingled the minute Jack Devlin arrived. Her breath backed up in her lungs and the tingling spread from her scalp, down her spine to the backs of her exposed bare legs.

She could feel those hot-chocolate eyes on her, no doubt dark with disapproval at her choice of attire for the occasion. Tough. Gerry had wanted a celebration of his life and that was what she'd arranged.

She might not have been Gerry Devlin's daughter by blood, but he had been her father in every other sense of the word, which gave her the right to do as she saw fit. His only offspring hadn't even had the courtesy to contact her about funeral arrangements.

Typical Jack Devlin. Too self-absorbed to think beyond his next conquest. Her lip curled. More than likely he'd been bonking some bimbo while his father lay dying.

But she didn't feel tough. She felt uncommonly fragile. Through sheer will, or plain old desperation, she restored her smile while she tugged ineffectually at the hem of her dress, then reached up to kiss Ben's cheek. 'Thank you for everything. Gerry would've enjoyed the send-off.'

'A pleasure, Cleo. Anything you need, just name it.' Ben's warm hands clasped her suddenly clammy ones and squeezed. She wanted to hang on, just a moment more—*please*—but his eyes flicked to the door, and her heart jolted. 'I'll be…it's Jack!'

Sucking in a breath, she braced herself. And turned.

But the dishevelled man a few feet away wasn't the fashion-savvy, smooth-cheeked Jack Cleo remembered. Oh, his broad shoulders still blocked the doorway and he still oozed that lazy, raw sexuality. Nor had his dark eyes—make that dark, bloodshot eyes—lost that uncanny knack of appearing hot and cold at the same time.

'Jack, my boy, it's good to see you.'

Ben's booming voice broke the spell she seemed to find herself under. Jack's gaze lingered on her a second longer, then switched to the man beside her.

'I'm only sorry it's under these circumstances,' Ben continued. 'My condolences.'

Jack nodded. 'Thank you.'

Rooted to the spot, Cleo watched them come together and shake hands.

Jack hadn't bothered to shave and he looked as if he'd just left a lover's bed. Unkempt dark hair curled over his collar. His trousers looked as if they'd been slept in, although she didn't imagine Jack slept in anything but a tan.

And did he think that stubble on his jaw was sexy? But her palm itched to touch; she could almost feel the roughness beneath her fingers... Heat rose up her neck and into her cheeks. Lucky for her both men were too busy talking to notice.

If the Jack she knew left stubble on his jaw, it was a skilful designer shadow. One that highlighted that dimple in his chin. The dimple she'd loved to touch just to annoy him. Of course that was before she'd become aware of him as a man rather than a brother—which he wasn't. But there was no mistaking the fact that Jack Devlin was all man.

Once again Jack's attention focused on her.

'I'll let you two get reacquainted,' she heard Ben say as he moved away.

She wasn't sure if the sound of music and conversation behind her dimmed. They simply ceased to exist. All she could hear was her pulse drumming in her ears, all she was aware of was the thick pounding of her heart against her chest. And Jack.

Drawing a deep breath, she forced her legs to move but stopped a safe arm's length away. *Safe?* His unfathomable eyes all but devoured her. She watched them roam her face, felt them as surely as a touch—brow, eyes, cheeks. Lips… If she hadn't known better she could have sworn—

But no. He hadn't come back for her. He'd come back for his father.

She willed away the humiliating sting of tears. *Hasn't he hurt you enough already? He doesn't think of you that way, never has, never will.*

He smelled of the aircraft, new shirt and unfamiliar soap, but underneath she smelled the scent unique to him. The scent that had invaded her dreams for too many years.

Clenching her fists at her sides so he wouldn't see the tremor, she lifted her chin. Even though she wore platform shoes he towered over her. 'So, the prodigal son returns.'

'Hello, Cleo.' Perhaps because it was expected of family, he touched his lips to her cheek. Her breath caught, then trembled out at that first physical contact. Unlike that final fevered and furious night in his room, his kiss was cool and detached.

But no less devastating.

To compensate, she waved a careless hand behind her. 'You're too late.'

'How ironic.' He was still leaning intimately towards her. His lips were smiling, and a casual observer might have thought he was pleased to see her, but his eyes were like granite. 'You said those exact same words the last time I saw you.'

At his twenty-first birthday party.

The night was indelibly printed into her brain. Sam Denton's bloodied nose when Jack had punched him through the car window, his fury as he'd dragged her from Sam's car. The shame when his father had caught Jack hustling her upstairs to his room with his jacket covering her open blouse and bare breasts.

And that final humiliation… She'd gotten the reaction she'd wanted all right, and paid the price. Her attempts to make Jack notice her, just once, had driven him out of her life.

'Or perhaps you were lying that night,' he murmured.

His voice catapulted her back to the present and the reality that he was going to throw all those old hurts in her face when what he *should* be asking about was his father.

He leaned closer. 'Was I?'

'Were you…what?'

'Too late.'

'What are you talking about?'

His voice was even enough but his expression held no hint of amusement. 'Convenient amnesia, Cleo?'

A fist slammed into her stomach. Amnesia would be a blessing. 'You're one to talk about "too late".' His sheer nerve, bringing up *that* night at his father's funeral, made her voice clipped and hard. 'You denied a dying man—a man I loved even if you didn't—his last wish.'

'Which was?'

'To say goodbye to you.'

Something dark and disturbing flickered in his eyes. But not guilt, not even regret. 'I came as soon as I heard.' His voice was rock-hard, like the set of his jaw.

Probably true, but it didn't let him off the hook. No way. She gave him her best impression of 'do I look stupid to you?'—pouted lips, lifted brow, a look she'd perfected years ago that never failed to provoke the heck out of him.

'If you don't mind, *Goldilocks*...' he retaliated in kind as he moved to collect his bag '...I'll dump my gear and wash up. Is my old room still my old room?'

How long had it been since she'd heard that pet name? And hated it?

Since Jack.

Determined not to make it easy for him to simply slip back into her life, she shrugged. 'If you can still find your way.'

As he bent to pick up his bag he staggered again, what little colour he had beneath his stubble leaching from his face. Cleo looked closer. His lips suddenly looked like chalk, the skin around them white and drawn. Alarmed, she fought her immediate response to lay a hand against his sweat-sheened brow and kept her voice impersonal. 'What's wrong with you? Are you sick?'

'Never better,' he said, gripping his bag in one white-knuckled fist. 'Give me fifteen minutes.' The corner of his mouth tipped up in a semblance of that cocky grin that had always set her teenage heart racing.

She'd vowed never again to let that mouth get to her, but her body wasn't paying attention. There was an industrial-strength blender in her stomach whipping up a deadly cocktail of unwanted emotions, forcing her to press a surreptitious fist against her middle.

She drew in a slow, deep breath. To her relief he turned on his heel and walked—make that sauntered—towards the hall as if the last six years hadn't happened.

Some things never changed. And there was still enough of the old Jack to have her traitorous system humming. Against her will, her eyes followed his firmly muscled backside as he disappeared through the doorway.

She curbed the swift desire to scream something obscene at him and screwed her eyes shut. She didn't need him in her life. Not now, not ever. She was going to focus on herself for a change, *her* wants, *her* needs. Forget Jack.

But her eyes flew open at the sound of a heavy thump followed by a short, sharp word, and her breath caught in her throat. Easy to say when the man was stumbling up the stairs like a drunk.

Mumbling an 'excuse me a moment' to anyone within earshot, she hurried into the hall and up the stairs. She stopped at the top and huffed out a breath. Back a few minutes and already he had her running after him. Again.

When she reached his door he was standing at the window, hands braced on the sill, taking deep breaths. She was three steps into the room before she could think that this was a very bad move. It hit her immediately. His scent, his proximity. The intimacy.

Back up. Now. But her feet remained stapled to the floor, eyes glued to his long, tanned fingers as he picked up her Champlevé enamel and bronze sculpture from the little bureau beneath the window.

'Did you make this?'

She bit her lip. He had his back to her, but he'd known she was there. He always knew. 'Yes,' she said finally. 'I've got my own workshop in the garage.'

'Impressive.' He set it down, turned around to check out the room.

His colour had improved, but he still had that greenish tinge. She felt a little faint herself. He was sucking up all the oxygen, taking up all the space. Even with the breeze and the fragrance of frangipani and wattle outside, she wondered if she was going to be the one passing out.

'New quilt,' he said.

Her eyes flicked to the burgundy and green patchwork, then away. She did not want to look at that bed. 'I sewed it at Gerry's bedside,' she said, focusing on the cool blank wall dead ahead and reminding herself Jack hadn't been around to see his dad die. 'It helped pass the time.'

The sudden image of Jack's naked body sliding over those patches she'd sewn burst like a fireball behind her eyes. All that hot, tanned skin rubbing against where her fingers had been… *Oh, Good God.*

Twisting those fingers together, she spun a half-circle, only to come face to face with the object of her steamy imaginings.

While she stared in helpless fascination, Jack

dragged off his tie, tossed it on the bed and unbuttoned a cuff. More hot, tanned skin. 'The old house has seen a few changes,' he remarked.

No thanks to him, she reminded herself again. 'You've been gone six years, Jack. You ran off without a word.'

The brief, mildly civilised interlude disintegrated into a deafening silence. Jack's fingers, already working the second cuff, paused. 'First off, I did not run.' A muscle clenched in his jaw. 'Second, it was time to leave.'

His eyes fused with hers and she knew they were both remembering... She knew what he meant even if she didn't understand why he'd left. 'But without saying goodbye?' They'd shared the shock and grief of losing a parent who'd never looked back—he *knew* how deeply that had hurt. He owed her. 'We deserved that much, your father at the very least.'

'Dad?' Something like anger or regret or both flashed in his eyes as he yanked open the top button of his shirt. 'He said what he had to say.'

She gulped, her eyes riveted to the glint of gold chain at his neck. The crudely shaped medallion nestling in that tempting V of chest had been one of her first attempts in metal-working class in high school.

He still wore it. Something fluttered at her heart, but she fought it down. 'He was your father, Jack. You treated him less than a stranger.'

'You more than made up for it.'

The sharp edge to his voice stung. Did he resent her for that?

'Speaking of parents,' he continued in a more reasonable tone, 'I didn't see your mum downstairs.'

Relieved at the switch in topics, Cleo nodded. 'She met someone through work and got married again.'

'Good for her.' He undid his belt, dropped it on the bed with his tie. 'She deserves some happiness.'

'I agree. They went to New Zealand to meet his family and stayed. She sent her condolences. By the way, I moved out of the flat to be nearer to Gerry since Mum's no longer around.' *And neither were you.*

His brows shot up. 'You cared for him yourself? Here?'

'Of course. When he wasn't having chemo.'

'Did you have help?' One hand shot up and rubbed at the back of his neck, the way she remembered he did when he was unsure of something. 'For God's sake tell me you didn't have to go through his…'

The 'death' word hung unspoken between them. 'I did have a carer help out at the end.' She wanted to reach out, but he deserved to suffer as she had. 'I did what I had to do. Death's part of being human.'

He nodded, still rubbing his neck. 'Big responsibility to take on.'

As if he would know about responsibility. 'Not at all. He was my father in all the ways that count.'

'The Dastardly Duo didn't know what they were throwing away when they left you behind.'

'That was fifteen years ago. I'm over it.' In a familiar but now almost unconscious reaction, she folded defensive arms across her breasts. Despite her plea to the contrary, she'd never been able to come to grips with her own father and Jack's mother running off together.

'Their loss, Goldilocks.' His voice mellowed, a warm, aged-whisky kind of sound that seemed to flow over her. She could almost feel her bones melting under his temperature-elevating gaze. She didn't even care that he'd used her old nickname.

Then he laid a hand on her shoulder, a move obviously neither of them had expected because she felt his fingers tense and heard her own soft inhalation. His hand moved to her neck, the rough edge of his fingertip catching on the silky fabric of her dress. Heat from his hard palm warmed the flesh of her exposed shoulder.

What was she thinking, letting him touch her as if he *cared*, as if he were absorbing the feel of her skin against his, searching her eyes for her deepest, darkest secrets? Simple. She wasn't thinking. Oh, my, but she was feeling. Her senses were so acutely tuned she swore she heard the air sigh. Or perhaps it was her. Or him.

It would be too easy to imagine that touch was more than what she knew it must mean: brotherly support. But his hand slid down, closed around her upper arm. Then both hands, both arms. Not brotherly at all.

A *thunk* downstairs followed by loud male laughter broke the sensual spell that had settled around them. Jack dropped his hands as if he'd touched molten metal. 'You've still got guests.'

The sudden loss of contact was a cold dash of reality. 'Correction—*we've* still got guests.' Rubbing her arms where the imprint of his hands still tingled, she said, 'This is your home, Jack, whether you like it or not, and those people downstairs came to say goodbye to your father.'

'With the exception of Ben, I didn't recognise a soul down there. Where's Jeanne? And Scotty said he'd be here.'

'Jeanne left early and Scott's performing a duty *you* should be doing. He's taking Moira home. Your second cousin once removed,' she reminded him, when he looked at her blankly.

'Ah, the bird lady. The one who talks like her galahs. Thank you, Scotty,' he murmured with a visible shudder.

She shook her head. 'I know more about your relatives than you do.' And that, she thought, said a lot about Jack's attitude towards family.

'You always did. Okay, I'll be down in ten minutes. Right now I've got a date with a hot shower.'

He yanked his shirt-tails out of his trousers and began undoing the rest of his buttons. The sight of that tempting strip of masculine skin had her stomach jigging in anticipation. What would happen if she touched him now, there? With her hands, her lips. With her tongue.

Reality check. Jack was off limits, for her own protection, and that included the scenery. She jerked her eyes back to his.

'So…if you'll excuse me?' Jack had paused, hands on the open sides of his shirt.

'Right.' Turning her back on him, she steeled her

mind to blank out all thoughts involving skin and hands and heat and said, 'I'll see you downstairs.'

The moment the last guest departed, Cleo kicked off her shoes before clearing up while she waited for Scott. He was coming back to check on her before heading home. Ben Hargreaves' son, Scott, and Jack might be best mates from high school, but Scott had been there for her from day one. Which made him the number-one hero in her books.

Forty-five minutes later she swung around as Scott's hands settled on her shoulders. She smiled. 'Hi.' This was more like it. No awkward silences, no shivering nerves getting in the way.

'Sorry I took so long. Moira wanted to show me the aviary. I'm not sure it's legal—all those cockatoos.'

'Galahs. She's lonely. Thanks for taking her home.' Cleo patted his cheek. 'Jack's back.' She heard the breathless sound of her own voice. To compensate, she moved briskly to the bench and busied herself covering leftovers with foil.

'Jack?' His voice brightened. 'Where is he?'

'Upstairs, said he was going to take a shower.' She glanced at the ceiling. 'That was more than an hour ago.' The thread of anxiety that had wound its way through her system tightened. She'd managed to ignore it until now, but, 'Perhaps I should go see if—'

'He'll show when he's ready—or not. You know Jack.'

She hesitated. 'You're right. It's just that…'

Scott leaned forward, cupped her chin in his hands.

Concern darkened his pale grey eyes, turning them pewter. 'You okay?'

'Fine. Why wouldn't I be?' But she pulled away, irritated to find her chest tight.

'Because you've always been hung up on him. Seeing him again is bound to be a bit of a jolt after all this time.'

Was it so obvious to everyone but Jack? With a harsh metallic *swoosh* she ripped more foil from the roll. '*Hung up* on him? Is that what you think? You're wrong.'

'Am I?'

'Yes.' On a crazy impulse, she tossed the foil roll on the bench and grabbed his shirt front. 'Kiss me, Scott. Really kiss me and I'll prove it to you.'

'Whoa, there.' He smiled and ran a thumb over her lips, presumably to take the sting out of his rejection. 'That's pure emotion talking.'

Of course it was. Jack and emotion went hand in hand. Her cheeks hot, she stepped back, picked up a platter of mini quiches and took them to the fridge. 'I'm sorry. That was stupid.'

'Forget it.' His smile widened fractionally. 'Another reason is self-preservation. I bet Jack's still protective of his little sister.'

'I'm *not* his sister.' She slammed the fridge door as irritation niggled through her. 'And I'm not so little any more.'

'Hey. Fine, sorry.' He raised his palms. 'You're *not* his sister. And you've got a thing for him.'

Thing. As in an itch? She shook her head. 'If only it were that simple.'

'The last time you saw him you were a kid. That would have made a relationship between you impossible—from Jack's point of view, at least. Now it's different and you don't know how to deal with it.'

'Is that why you never put the moves on me? Because you knew?' *Way to go, Cleo—put Scott in a no-win situation.* 'Sorry, personal question. Forget I said that.'

He nodded. 'Forgotten.' He picked up his keys, jingled them. 'You still on for tomorrow night?'

'On?'

'As in basketball.'

'Oh.' She pasted on a smile. 'Right.'

'We're playing the bottom team; it should be a walkover. I'll let myself out.' But he didn't give her his customary kiss goodbye. 'See you tomorrow.'

'Bye.' She leaned one burning cheek against the smooth fridge until the sound of Scott's car faded. Cricket song filtered through the open window. She heard a dog bark against the background of traffic, felt the cool dampness of evening on her heated skin.

Only an idiot would yearn half a lifetime for a playboy like Jack over a steady, dependable guy like Scott. A sigh slid from her lips. Scott had been there for her when Gerry's time had come. Jack was his son; where had *he* been?

If the clipping at the bottom of her underwear drawer was any indication, he'd been living the high life in Italy. She knew the words by heart. 'And in Milan, Mr Jack Devlin, up-and-coming fashion photographer, escorting Ms Liana Kumova, a stunning, new...'

Cleo snorted, unsure who she was more disgusted with—Jack or herself for allowing it to still hurt.

What else had Mr Jack Model-a-Minute done in the past six years?

And how long would he stay this time?

CHAPTER TWO

TIME. Cleo glanced at the digital numbers on the microwave. Jack hadn't made that promised appearance downstairs. The one person who might have understood her grief, who might have shared it, simply didn't care.

Pushing away from the fridge, she headed for the stairs. Forget that the earth still moved when she looked at him, that the brush of a fingertip over her skin had sent shock waves rippling through every pulse-point in her body. A normal physical response to an attractive male.

But this attractive male wasn't the man she wanted him to be. Not inside, where it counted. She didn't want him on those terms. *You keep telling yourself that, Cleo. Maybe one day you'll even believe it.*

And while she waited for that little miracle to happen, she intended letting him in on a few home truths. Hers.

Jack's door was ajar, the room dark. The last vestige of dusk slid through the open drapes, outlining a motionless form sprawled over the lower half of the bed.

She slapped a palm on the door, swinging it wide. 'Jack, wake up. I want to talk to you.'

No answer.

From the doorway she could hear his steady breathing. Her own breath caught as the sound of that gentle rumble skated down her spine and the backs of her legs. God help her, she should leave. Now. Before he woke and found her watching him like some star-struck teenager. 'Jack…'

When he still didn't stir, she slipped into the room. She had to make a conscious effort to put one foot in front of the other as she crossed the carpet to switch on the bedside lamp. She adjusted it to its dimmest setting.

It looked as if he'd fallen backwards onto the quilt and hadn't budged since. His open shirt revealed a patina of sun-bronzed skin sprinkled with cinnamon hair that gleamed gold in the low light. A metal-smith's divine inspiration—she could almost feel the flow of molten metal beneath her fingers. It took all her willpower to keep her hands at her sides.

His chain had slipped to the side, the medallion nestled between neck and shoulder. But she frowned at the ugly bruise blooming on the left side of his chest. Then she noticed the bulky surgical dressing over his shoulder just visible beneath his shirt.

'What have you done to yourself this time, Jack?'

He wore bruises like badges, she remembered, always getting into fights, more than likely over some girl or other. This was probably no exception.

She brushed his unruly hair from his forehead. His

brow was cool and smooth—no fever—and she had no business touching him, except that she'd always been a sucker when Jack was hurt.

More fool her.

But worry worked its way through the euphoric haze that seemed to have enveloped her and she gently shook his uninjured shoulder. 'Jack?'

He jerked, eyes suddenly wide and glassy and unfocused. 'Huh?'

'It's Cleo, Jack.' His eyelids slipped to half-mast at the sound of her voice, those dark bedroom eyes barely visible through spiky lashes. She had the weirdest sensation of falling. 'Are you okay?' Leaning closer, she could smell the warm, sleepy scent of his skin. 'Do you need anything?' *Like me.*

For a heart-stopping instant she thought she must have spoken those two reckless words aloud when he murmured, 'Cleo...' then his eyes closed on the word '...Home...'

She sighed. Not a chance—the words 'Cleo' and 'home' did not equate in Jack's vocabulary. Leastways, not in this lifetime.

Deliberately ignoring the unsnapped waistband of his trousers, she detoured to the foot of the bed, tugged off his shoes, then peeled off his socks, sucking in a breath as her fingers came into contact with warm, bony skin.

His bare feet stuck out over the edge of the mattress. Long, narrow feet... God, even his toes were sexy; in a knobbly kind of way. She shook her head in exasperation. Only Jack Devlin could have sexy toes.

She grabbed a light blanket from a chest of drawers and draped it over his inert body. Obviously he wasn't going to surface any time soon.

'Oh, Jack,' she whispered, sinking into the armchair beside the bed. 'We had so many good times when we were kids. You were my best friend. You didn't even get mad when I soldered your meccano set to make a windmill.'

She smiled at the memory, but the smile faded as quickly as it came. 'Why did everything change?'

It had been in this room, she thought, staring at the window. The evening started off okay. The Plan had been to give Jack her virginity and he'd see they were meant for each other. Only the Plan had gone horribly wrong.

Not only had Jack backed away from her when the CD had started a slow dance number, he'd started drinking. A lot. Hurt, she'd flirted with Sam and somehow they'd ended up in the back seat of his car with a bottle of vodka.

Until Jack's fist had appeared through the car window.

The memory struck hard. Unable to sit, Cleo stood and paced the carpet. That night she'd been standing here hugging her arms the same way, but for an entirely different reason. Her new blouse with its tiny front-closing loop buttons had been hanging open, her bra missing.

The party lights outside cast Jack's rock-hard face in an orange glow. Over the ringing in her ears she could hear raucous laughter and loud music.

Jack's fingers dug into the flesh of her upper arms, dark eyes flashing with something so much more dangerous than temper. 'What the hell have you done?'

'What do you care?' Cleo tried to dash the wetness from her eyes but Jack kept her arms pinned to her sides, easily holding her in place.

'You're sixteen, Cleo. Do you know what that means?'

Right now all she knew was she wanted to scream, to pummel him, to throw herself at that broad chest and beg him to make love to her. But that wasn't going to happen. She knew that now. 'I hate you, Jack Devlin. I'm going to find someone who'll show me a good time.' Her lips stretched into a sneer. 'A very good time.'

His fingers tightened, and the look on his face made her shudder with something close to fear. 'You want a good time?' he said between clenched teeth, the words barely audible over the blood pulsing through her cotton-wool head.

His mouth crushed down on hers, hot, hard and unforgiving. She couldn't pull away because his hand had hold of her scalp. Barely able to stand, she stood frozen as his lips mashed against hers, his teeth cutting into the soft flesh inside her lower lip. His tongue plunged through her lips, open with shock.

Then he jerked away, breath ragged and rasping, eyes tormented, his beautiful lips glistening in the dim light. Then he swiped a hand across his mouth as if her taste were poison and strode towards the door. 'You've got two minutes to make yourself presentable and be out of my sight or I won't be responsible for my actions.'

'You're too late, Big Brother,' she shouted at his retreating back.

'I'll kill him,' she heard him say as he slammed the door behind him.

Closing her eyes briefly, Cleo drew the curtain on those memories. She blew a long breath and rubbed her cheeks. Then turned to look at Jack. Still sleeping, thank God.

Jack had made it clear how he'd felt about her six years ago. He'd kissed her and it had disgusted him. He'd been so disgusted he'd threatened her with dire consequences. She hadn't seen or heard from him since.

Leaving the night lamp on, she slipped towards the door. The image of Jack on her patchwork quilt had burned into her brain and warmed up a few erogenous zones besides.

In spite of everything, she still wanted him. 'Sweet dreams, Jack,' she whispered into the semi-darkness. *On second thought make that not-so-sweet dreams.*

Jack knew he was dreaming but that didn't make it less real. His head twisted from side to side, his breathing picked up pace. The sky was bone-white, the land baked and brown. And cold. He shivered as the wind whistled through his sweat-damp shirt, and hefted another boulder from what had once been a simple home.

He could hear a woman wailing, but the ragged

children were silent ghosts watching him out of dark, hollowed eyes in dirt-stained faces. Their village was a pile of rubble. The dead stank.

Then out of nowhere, gunfire and screams. The white-hot sting of metal piercing flesh, the thud as his body hit hard-packed dirt. He writhed on the ground, biting dust while his blood trickled hot over his skin. *Get down! Get down!*

Darkness engulfed him. And somewhere in that dark place filled with pain a familiar voice spoke his name. That hadn't happened in the dream before. He tried to open his eyes to see her but they were glued shut.

Cool hands touched his face, stroked his arms. He smelled jasmine as she stretched out alongside him.

Then stillness, and a tranquillity that went soul deep…

He must have died and gone to heaven. A hazy memory of an angel teased the edges of his mind. A less-than-holy angel with a siren's voice and one hell of a bedside manner. And he could still smell the jasmine… He frowned. Angels wore perfume?

He opened his eyes and found her. A tousled and sleeping angel named Cleo curled up on the armchair beside him. He noticed an indent on the adjacent pillow confirming that at some stage Cleo had lain beside him.

Like a gunshot, something inside him pinged as images of her flooded back. The Cleo he remembered was always moving, a blur of colour and energy. So it was a rare and beautiful sight to see her still and innocent in sleep with the subtle bloom of sunrise on her cheeks, the disorderly halo of golden hair around her face.

But her mouth, relaxed and full—he thought of a plump red cherry. Why did the word *ripe* seem so apt? Perhaps it had something to do with the fact that he'd spent so many years remembering the absolute innocence of her taste and wondering if it had matured.

She sighed as if responding to his thoughts, but her eyes remained shut. She'd covered herself from neck to toes in a cotton sheet. Just as well because he knew the body beneath was way too distracting for a man barely out of hospital, let alone a man who didn't fit in with her life.

Unfortunately his imagination wasn't impaired. Neither was his testosterone. His blood grew thick and sluggish, pooling in his groin. With a harsh sigh he shoved the cover down to his waist, closed his eyes and concentrated on the cool air moving over his chest and face.

Come on, Jack. Think of her as just another photo shoot. Except she'd never be model material. Not enough self-discipline, too small in stature, too many curves. The thought of those delicate curves had his mind wandering in a direction he didn't want to go.

Instead, he set his mind to imagining her *covered* in silk; peach, the colour of her skin. Or reclining in a wheelbarrow, covered in leaves—only leaves, the colour of autumn to match the gold glints in her hair.

But he couldn't get past the image of a crisp autumn wind playing havoc, undoing his artistic handiwork, her rosy nipples pebbly with the chill…

Jack swore silently. He needed a distraction. A run was out; the alternative was a cold shower. He ordered his sluggish body to move, but his legs refused to obey. An instant of pure panic sliced through him.

His eyes shot to the foot of the bed. The small mountain of white fur on his calves seemed to augment as the animal, he assumed it was, uncurled itself. A pair of eyes—one gold, one green—opened, blinked once in disdain, then slid shut. '*What* is that?' he muttered, exhaling on a breath of relief.

'*Who,*' Cleo corrected.

He glanced her way. Coupled with the amusement sparkling in her eyes, her sleep-husky voice conspired to crumble his already-damaged resolve. He looked back at the bottom of the bed and scowled. '*Who*, then?'

'His name's Constantine and he's a very spoilt, very arrogant Persian-cross, but he thinks he's human.'

'What the dickens do you feed him? He's massive.'

'Seven kilos at the last weigh-in. Come on, Con.' An ominous rumble vibrated against Jack's feet as Cleo shoved her sheet off and rose. 'Uh-oh, temper alert. Watch.'

But all Jack could focus on was the tantalising way Cleo's breasts swayed beneath her tiny vest-top with its star-and-moon print as she leaned over him and reached for the cat.

There was an indignant growl and a flurry of loose cat fur as she heaved the white mass onto the floor. Shaking back her hair, Cleo watched him stalk off, tail bristling like a feather duster. 'Trouble is he usually sleeps with me.'

Lucky Con. 'Must get a little crowded.'

Her skin flushed from peach to rose. Grabbing the sheet, she pulled it tight around her like some sort of cotton armour and something more than anger fired those eyes to a hot blue flame. 'You know nothing about me or my life. You never bothered to keep in contact. That makes my social life none of your business.'

Did she think he was suggesting *crowded* as in *bed*? 'I only meant…' He didn't want to know her sleeping habits, wanted to think about it even less. 'Forget it.'

She'd been manipulating boys since reaching puberty at thirteen. It had been a recurring headache, keeping one eye on the rebellious teen and one on her male admirers, and never the twain shall meet. At age twenty-two presumably she had it down pat now.

He rolled to his side, stuck his uninjured hand behind his head and asked, 'Have you been here all night?'

'You were obviously having a nightmare. I was just going to bed and I wanted to check you were all right…' She lifted her chin. 'I fell asleep. If you think it was for any other reason, you're sicker than I thought.'

But she'd thought about it enough to have gotten herself a sheet. In some ways she hadn't changed. The same caring nature inside the same prickly shell. A smile touched his lips. 'A few days' rest and I'll be fine, but thank you.'

That chin jutted up a notch. 'No big deal; I'm used to sleeping upright. I often slept at Gerry's bedside.'

Her matter-of-fact retort came armed with a barb aimed squarely at him. And she'd be right on target. She'd borne a responsibility that had belonged to Jack Devlin.

He wanted to think that if he'd known about his father's illness earlier he'd have come home, that he'd have made some sort of peace with him, but the scars in their relationship ran bone-deep. If he had come, it would have been for Cleo's sake, not Dad's.

'He used to like me to read to him till he fell asleep,' she said softly. 'In the early hours when the pain got bad...' Eyes brimming, she sniffed and grabbed a tissue from the nightstand, but her glare warned him she'd more likely take a chunk out of him than not if he offered any kind of comfort.

So he stayed as he was and asked, 'How long was Dad ill?'

'That a son would have to ask that question.' She shook her head. 'He knew it was terminal two years ago. It didn't get too bad until the last three months—they were hard on both of us, but he wanted to die at home.' Her moisture-laden eyes pinned him to the mattress. 'He wanted *you* here when he died.'

Jack felt the sting of her words as surely as if she'd run him through with one of those metal-smithing tools he'd seen her wield. But the belligerent man Cleo had never seen because Dad had ensured his temper had remained behind closed doors hadn't been the type to apologise. Which left him wondering what they'd have had to say to each other.

'I'm sorry, Goldilocks.'

Cleo stared at him and in the silence he swore the

temperature plummeted. She blew her nose sharply, then walked to the adjoining bathroom to dispose of the tissue, trailing the sheet behind her. 'It wasn't me asking for you,' she said when she reappeared.

If Cleo had contacted him, he'd have made the effort. He'd have moved heaven and earth. For her. But Jack himself had made that connection impossible. 'I didn't know he was dying.'

'And whose fault's that?'

His. Scotty, the only person he'd kept contact with, hadn't let him know. Jack didn't hold him responsible; the blame lay with Jack for not asking. 'Why didn't you hire a nurse sooner?'

'A nurse?' Her eyes flashed again as she hugged the sheet tighter. 'A nurse isn't a substitute for family. *Family*, Jack. But you wouldn't know about that, would you?

'One day, Jack Devlin, you're going to be sorry you turned your back on the people closest to you, the people who care about you, even when they didn't know where the hell you were because you never bothered to write or call or let us know.'

There wasn't much of her, but the raw edge to her anger packed a punch that reverberated all the way to his toes. He'd known she was strong—stubborn was the word he'd used. But now, with her maturity, he could see so much more. Loyalty, for starters.

He deserved every word she hurled at him. Not on Dad's account—Jack would never regret his decision to leave. For not being here for Cleo, for not making contact with her, for causing her pain.

But she'd never seen the whole picture. She'd been

looking through the lens while the action had taken place behind the camera.

He wanted to keep it that way. 'Sometimes things aren't as black and white as you think.'

'You're no better than the parents who walked out on us. In fact, you're worse because you know first-hand how it feels to be abandoned.'

His temple was beginning to throb again and he had no idea when he'd last eaten. 'Cleo, I don't want to fight about this now. If you'll excuse me, I'm going to take that overdue shower.'

'And I need coffee.' She paused at the door. 'Do you require any help with that dressing on your shoulder? And that bruise...' Her eyes slid over his body and away. 'Did you see a doctor?'

'I can manage, and yes.'

'Was she worth it?' Her gaze snapped back to his, as frosty as her voice.

She? 'What makes you think I was with a woman?'

Cleo laughed, a brittle sound that skittered along his bones like chipped ice. 'Try: your reputation. I assume you took it with you when you left?'

'Wouldn't leave home without it.' And it suited him fine to let her think so.

But the deceptive laziness he projected was a stark contrast to the tension stiffening his shoulders and neck as he watched her. Not to mention other body parts stiffening in response to the sight of a tanned bare thigh peeking out from behind her sheet shield. Her wide legged jersey shorts didn't quite cover the curve of one very cute, well-rounded buttock.

'Just because I left home doesn't mean I didn't think about you.' He immediately cursed himself. Why had he said that?

'Yeah, right.' She glared at him, her mouth compressed to a grim line, at odds with the soft play of sunlight over her face. She crossed the room again, coffee obviously forgotten. 'I stopped thinking about *you* a long time ago.'

But just for a second her eyes had that same little-girl-lost look he'd seen when her father had announced he'd fallen in love with Jack's mother, both archaeologists, and they were leaving on a dig in two days. Cleo had been seven years old.

His parents had rented out the flat adjacent to the house to his mum's colleague from uni. They'd become more than colleagues.

From that day on Cleo hadn't spoken a word about her biological father. It was as if she'd buried him. Jack understood her pain. After all, it had been his own mother the bastard had run off with.

Had she buried Jack Devlin in the same dark hole? Not that he blamed her, particularly after the fiasco of that last night... Moving carefully, he sat up, swung his legs over the bed and planted his feet on the carpet. 'Cleo—'

'Don't.' She held up a hand. 'Don't say a word.' Her sheet drifted further apart, giving him a close-up of taut, smooth skin between the hem of her mini top and those sinfully short shorts. Not to mention the shadowed top of one inner thigh. He took a fortifying breath and reluctantly shifted his eyes to hers.

'You're history, Jack. You may think you're God's gift to women, but not to *this* woman. This woman wants more than a quick roll between the sheets and a kiss goodbye.'

The thought of a naked Cleo in bed with some faceless man was a black hole he always took pains to steer clear of. 'I damn well hope so.'

She nodded, aimed a thumb at her chest. 'Good. Because this woman wants a man who's not afraid to stick around for the family and commitment bit.'

Two of the words he feared most. 'I'm not big on family and commitment. I learned from the best.'

Cleo snorted. 'I was there too, remember, and I haven't inherited your aversion. Don't blame others for your inadequacies, or your fears.' A disgruntled meow and the sound of claws sharpening on upholstery somewhere in the hall interrupted her. 'I'd better let Con out. Like most males I know, he thinks the world revolves around him.'

Jack waited till she left before easing off the bed. 'Whoa.' Dizziness surged through him and he sat down again, clamped his hands to the mattress and took slow deep breaths. A few minutes to get his bearings and he'd be right. Nothing some good Aussie tucker and a couple of painkillers wouldn't cure. He was home, safe and *almost* sound.

Home. The word slipped subtly into his mind before he realised. He'd taken great care not to use the term, because it invariably engulfed him in memories he'd wanted to forget. Now here he was. Swamped.

Thank God for his camera. Freelancing the world

had kept his focus off what he couldn't have and directed it down more productive paths. Four years ago he'd traded glitz and glamour for war zones, lived for the present and refused to think beyond his current assignment. It was better than beating himself up over what he couldn't change.

His current assignment was sorting out Dad's finances and selling the house.

Not as straightforward as he'd imagined. Pushing up slowly, he winced as stiff muscles protested. So Cleo was no longer in the flat. No, sir, she'd made herself quite at home in the house.

Shaking off the niggling discomfort at living in such close quarters with the girl he'd wanted almost for ever, he moved to the window and looked out at the rainbow-coloured rose garden below. She had every right to be here. She'd nursed his father and presumably seen to the upkeep of the house and the well-tended grounds while Dad's health had declined. Alone. He couldn't very well ask her to leave straight away.

He rubbed at the back of his neck. Perhaps she'd consider taking the flat again—rent-free of course. He could arrange for her to continue using the garage as a workshop until an alternative venue could be found.

Guilt speared up and lodged like a sharp splinter in his chest. Hell, he didn't even know whether she'd had to give up a job, if she sold any of the stuff she made, whether Dad had given her an allowance.

Nor did he want his father's wealth. Leastways not for himself. He'd put it towards the rebuilding efforts he'd been supporting overseas. As far as he could see, money came with a heap of its own problems, and he'd been doing fine on his own minus the complications.

But he owed Cleo. One hell of a complication. Until he figured out the best way to repay that debt, he was stuck here in the danger zone, and this time there was no airlift out in sight.

CHAPTER THREE

JACK took his time washing the sweat of travel from his skin. The steam felt like a balm to his body, the warmth easing stiff muscles. He felt almost human again. Until he wiped the moisture from the mirror with his palm.

He shook his head. 'You've looked better,' he muttered. Couldn't do much for the eyes, but he reached for his razor and began scraping away a few days' worth of beard.

That task completed, he gingerly peeled off the dressing on his shoulder. He could've used some help but the thought of Cleo's neat little hands anywhere near his flesh convinced him to deal with it himself. Not a pretty sight and the wound burned like a devil, but he cleaned and dressed it with one of the sterile packs from the hospital.

Finally he pulled on jeans and an old black T-shirt that was soft against his bruised body, and ran a comb through his overlong hair. He grimaced at his reflection. He'd *definitely* looked better.

He left his room and walked down the hall, his bare

feet almost noiseless on the smooth parquetry floor. He noted the walls were a warm cream rather than the austere white they'd always been. The stairs and banister gleamed and a fresh lingering fragrance of lemon polish mingled with the smell of coffee—and was that pizza?—and the homey sounds of clunking dishes and breakfast radio.

Two steps down, he stopped and stared at the statue at the base of the stairs. Spikes of metal speared and curled into sinuous curves, giving an impression of intertwined limbs, an unmistakable breast… How had he missed this piece of metallic erotica last night? One of Cleo's pieces, obviously.

'Now there's a face I haven't seen in a while.'

Jack turned at the sound of Scott's voice. 'Scotty!' His childhood buddy stood in the entry foyer, looking much smarter than the uni student he remembered, in a lightweight Armani suit and royal-blue tie. His liberal dousing of Calvin Klein wafted up the stairwell. Jack grinned as he descended. 'Still as ugly as ever.'

Scott grinned back. 'Not as ugly as you.' He crossed tiles in three strides and grasped both Jack's hands.

'Got to agree with you there.' Relief sighed through Jack at the open and uncomplicated welcome. 'So… what's with the clothes?'

'I'm on my way to a client.'

'Ah, of course. Scott the lawyer now. Father and son team.'

At the mention of family ties Scott paused, looking uncomfortable as he rocked back on the heels of his shiny black shoes. 'Sorry about your father.'

'Yeah.' Jack couldn't think of anything else to say.

'How's it feel to be back?'

'I'll let you know when my body catches up.'

Scott gave Jack a thorough once-over. 'You haven't changed much. Perhaps a bit leaner and meaner.' His eyes slid over Jack's hair. 'No scissors where you come from?'

Jack shoved a hand through damp strands. 'No time.'

'Jeanne can trim it. Sis has her own salon now.'

'Good for Jeanne.' But Jack was super aware of Cleo moving about in the kitchen and didn't want to be overheard. 'What's a hot-shot lawyer drive these days?'

'Jeep Cherokee Sports.'

'Let's take a look.' They wandered out the front door and down the path to the driveway where Scott's car gleamed silver in the sun.

Scott opened the car door, released the bonnet. Both men ostensibly studied the engine but Jack knew they had stuff to talk about. 'Had it long?' he asked.

'Four months.'

'I'll have to road test it some time.' Jack ran a hand over the bodywork. 'You didn't let on he was sick.'

'I took over some of Dad's clients when he had his heart attack; your father was one of them. He gave specific instructions about not trying to find you till it was over.'

Jack almost smiled. Dad hadn't filled Cleo in on that information. Jack could only presume his reason was to make him look like the heartless son. 'So he never knew we kept contact?'

'No. Nobody knew. Had to do some fast talking to our girl here. Told her I hired an investigator.' Scott shook his head. 'The Middle East, Jack. Every time I heard of a foreigner being kidnapped I thought of you.'

Jack shuddered inwardly at the blurred memories of the field hospital, the airlift to Rome when he'd stabilised enough to be moved, then forced a casual grin. 'Life on the edge.' No way did he want to relive the past couple of weeks, not even with Scotty.

'You make a habit of landing in hospital, then?'

'Not since I was here.' Again Jack's mind spun back to his twenty-first birthday, but this time it was the dark recollection of his father's fists.

'You should've pressed charges, Jack. Two broken ribs and multiple bruises. It wasn't the first time.'

'But it was the last.' He shrugged to cover the emotional pain that still stabbed through him at the memories. 'Forget it, it's in the past. Fill me in on Cleo.' At Jack's own request they'd never discussed her while he'd been away. He'd mistakenly thought it would distance her from his mind, from his heart. Wrong.

'She's fine,' Scott said. 'We've gotten close over the years.'

Jack's gut cramped at the unwelcome image that popped into his head. 'How close?'

Scott grinned. 'Told her you'd do the brotherly protection bit. We're friends, that's all.'

Jack shoved his hands behind his head and linked his fingers to ease the tension between his shoulder blades. 'You think she and Sam…?'

Scott laughed. 'After That Night? Hell, no.'

Jack imagined punching a triumphant fist in the air but remained outwardly calm. 'I think she hung around those types just to rile me.'

'She succeeded. You got into more than one fight on her account.'

'For all the good it did. She was a messed-up kid.'

Scott lowered the bonnet with a mechanical click and pierced Jack with a look that had Jack's outward calm ruffling at the edges. 'She's not a kid any more.'

Too right she wasn't, and it scared the living daylights out of Jack. 'I've already noticed she's more than capable of looking out for herself.'

'Are you guys coming in for breakfast or what?' Cleo called from the open doorway.

'Coming,' Scott called back and clapped Jack on the shoulder. 'Let's go eat.'

When Jack entered the familiar sunny yellow kitchen Cleo was unloading the dishwasher. She wore hip-hugging jeans with rainbow pockets and a shrunken violet vest-top that left a tantalising strip of midriff bare. The top stretched over her breasts surely tighter than would be comfortable. Her puckered nipples looked as if they needed rescuing.

He imagined putting his tongue in the curve of her waist, then working his way up, sliding his fingers under that snug fabric to ease her distress—and give him access to all that smooth skin and those two perky little buds.

She stopped in mid-stoop when she saw him looking. He caught her eyes, and for a brief second he thought he saw a flash of something intimate, then... nothing.

'Help yourself,' she said, closing the dishwasher.

He drew in a deep breath. Was it the smell of food or the sight of woman that had his juices flowing, his mouth watering? A lack of both had sharpened his senses and he aimed for the nearest chair and collapsed onto it.

He was right about the smell—it *was* pizza, along with mini quiches, toasted sandwiches and half a soggy pavlova loaded with strawberries and cream.

Scott seemed to know his way around their breakfast table and was already pouring coffee into mugs. 'You going to give Jeanne a try?'

'Why not?' Jack said, wondering if his taste buds could cope with pepperoni pizza this early in the morning on an empty stomach.

Scott pulled out his mobile phone.

'Good idea,' said Cleo, and sat down. Her arm, sprinkled with tiny gold hairs and smelling like jasmine, passed in front of Jack and hovered under his nose as she selected a toasted Vegemite sandwich. She cast a glance over his hair. 'Though it does give you a certain untamed appeal. Some women might find that attractive.'

She'd admired that untamed look six years ago, he remembered, though *feral* might be a more apt word for the guys she'd mixed with. It soured his mood and did nothing for his appetite. 'So you go for what—slick and sophisticated nowadays?' he said.

She snatched her hand back. 'Isn't that *your* preference?'

He felt the sharp edge to her voice like a knife between his ribs and paused, pizza poised halfway to his lips. Her expression wasn't any softer than her tone. Ignoring both, he bit off a mouthful and chewed, but the flavour had lost its spice.

What kind of man *did* she go for now? He'd resigned himself to the fact that she'd have had men in her life. But seeing the stunning woman she'd matured into, sharing the same air and breathing her scent… The thought of any man touching her peachy skin was an exercise in torture. And something he'd have to get used to fast.

'We weren't discussing me,' he said at last. 'Hopefully you've gotten some wisdom along with your maturity.' Now he was really starting to sound like a big brother.

'Your appointment's for ten,' Scott said, setting the phone down. 'Jeanne's looking forward to seeing you again.'

'Thanks, Scotty.'

'So, Jack.' Cleo sliced herself a generous serving of pavlova. 'Tell us about yourself. Rome, wasn't it? I think I read something about it in some magazine.' She lifted one shoulder, took a gulp of coffee. 'Photographing all those Italian beauties. Must be a hard life.'

'I—'

Scott's mobile buzzed. Scott spoke briefly, disconnected. 'Those Italian beauties will have to wait. I've got to run.' Rising, he drained his coffee. 'Cleo, can you take Jack to the mall later?'

She answered with a hesitant, 'Okay.'

Jack understood her reluctance and was tempted to cancel the whole business and go back to bed. Or perhaps she had someone else she wanted to be with today. 'I can find my own way,' he said, eyeing her over his mug. 'If you're expected elsewhere…'

He was dismissed with a curt, 'Don't be ridiculous, you're in no shape to drive. I'm taking you and that's that.' She shrugged as she licked cream from her fingers. 'I've nothing better to do.'

But as Jack watched Cleo clear and stack plates her quick and edgy movements let him know she'd agreed only as a favour to Scott. She still had that chip on her shoulder, though she'd smoothed the edges some. And he couldn't help thinking what a nice shoulder it was.

To distract himself from the sight of that trim body, he directed his gaze through the glassed doors that opened onto the patio, and beyond, to the bottom of the garden. 'The old wattle tree's still there.' Dense with foliage, it was still a perfect spot for a cubby or a cuddle…

'Where you got a little too friendly with a certain Sally Edwards,' Cleo reminded him.

'Thanks to you, one of my less memorable moments.' Unbeknown to him, Cleo had watched the proceedings from above, and just when things had been getting interesting she'd decked him with her shoe. Unfortunately Sally hadn't seen the humour in the situation.

Cleo turned to look at him. 'Remember that time I climbed higher than you?'

'An unfair contest—the branches didn't support my weight.'

'Ah, but you were taller. Bet you couldn't do it now.' Her voice held a definite sneer.

Jack recognised the old challenge, and met her eyes. 'That sounds suspiciously like a dare.'

She tossed out a laugh as she filled the sink. 'Hardly, for someone in your condition.'

But the triumph in her eyes was enough. 'You're on, but I've got something better.' And something a man recovering from concussion and assorted wounds probably shouldn't attempt, but pride was at stake here.

'Like what?' He saw the flicker of alarm in her eyes as he strode to the glass doors, slid them open. 'Coming?'

'Jack, wait.' His strides took him to the front of the house while Cleo sputtered behind him. 'Whatever you're planning, don't.'

Jack allowed himself a rare moment of light-headed amusement as he put one bare foot on the first rung and gauged his ascent up the trellis to his window while Cleo tugged at his arm, her nails pressing into his flesh. He liked the way she clung to him a little too much.

Definitely light-headed. Temporary insanity even. That was what he told himself as he planted a quick hard kiss on her parted mouth and swung up. 'If I fall, I want my ashes scattered on—'

'Shut up and get down or I'm going to kill you myself.'

His own lips tingling from the unexpectedly lush heat of Cleo's mouth, he gritted his teeth, wincing as pain sang through his body. 'Like riding a bike,' he muttered, picking his way through a forest of ivy. Virtually one-handed was only a minor handicap. He was fitter at this point in his life than he'd ever been.

But his head was spinning and he was sweating with a sudden dose of something he refused to consider as the shakes when he hauled himself through the window. Still, he managed a wave at a white-lipped Cleo below.

Then he flopped onto his back on the floor and closed his eyes. The room tilted. His shoulder screamed. The throbbing in his temple grew to epic proportions. *Don't pass out, for God's sake.*

But he didn't have time to enjoy his pain in solitude because in the next moment Cleo burst through his bedroom door and was bending over him, wild-eyed and spitting mad.

'You idiot!'

He would have smiled if he'd had the energy—it had been a long time since anyone had shown emotion of any kind towards him. He closed his eyes. 'Hi, Goldilocks. You made good time.'

'Shut up, Jack.'

Her voice was breathy, impatient. Like an aroused woman. Cool fingers slid his T-shirt up his chest, working gently over and along every tender rib. One, two, three...

His breath stalled in his lungs. It was too easy to imagine those fingers sliding lower, dipping beneath the waistband of his jeans. His suddenly very tight jeans. He might hurt more than he'd admit, but he wasn't dead. Yet.

'Piece of cake,' he told her, pushing up, mostly to

cover the incriminating evidence in his lap. The eyes that met his were stormy pools of blue. The light fragrance wafting from her skin made his head spin again for a different reason entirely. 'I used to do it regularly. Don't worry.'

'I wouldn't waste my time.' She pushed away the hand he'd automatically lifted to her cheek and stood, fisting her hands against her sides. 'We leave for the mall at nine forty-five. Don't be late.'

'I'll be ready.'

Not one of your more intelligent ideas, Jack, he thought, when he was alone again. Trouble was he'd quickly rediscovered that, where Cleo was concerned, emotion rode roughshod over sense.

Which didn't bode well for however long it took to settle Cleo in a place of her own, wrap things up and be gone.

Under an array of brilliant down-light, Hair's Jeanne was bustling with the sounds of scissors and dryers, the smells of shampoos and lotions.

An attractive brunette like her brother, Jeanne smiled from a distance while she put the finishing touches to a client's hair. But Cleo noted Jeanne's eyes were all for Jack this morning. And why not? The woman was alive, wasn't she?

Knowing it would be rude to take the single, safer chair on the opposite wall when there was a space beside him—even if it was a very small space—Cleo sat on his right.

Her arm was hard up against Jack's. Their jeans-clad thighs brushed. Obviously Jack didn't experience the same jolt that sent heat spiralling through her system. With a casual ease she envied, he picked up a periodical and began flicking through it.

It was impossible not to see his reflection in the salon mirrors. His eyes were on his magazine and all she could see were the long, dark lashes. And the dimple. And that mouth. He could have been in front of the camera instead of behind. She scowled. That might make him poster-boy material, but it didn't make him a better person.

So why did she feel so weak, so…hot? And what was she going to do about it?

Remember what he did.

Forcing her eyes away, she reached for distraction with a copy of *Cosmopolitan* and opened it at random. As Jack turned a page one hair-dusted forearm grazed hers, sending sparks of awareness shooting to her shoulder. *Hurry up, Jeanne.*

She needed a job, something part-time to get her by until she could earn enough with her jewellery and metalwork creations. She had a few shop owners taking orders on commission, and a few art pieces in a couple of galleries, but not enough to live on.

She flipped the page, looked closer. The woman in the picture wore a silver ensemble—G-string and feathers. She was gripping a pole with her thighs, one arm behind her head, fingers artfully rippling through her hair.

'Executive by day, stripper by night.' She hadn't realised she'd read aloud until Jack shifted a shoulder and glanced at her magazine.

'Can't they come up with something better than that?' he said.

But she saw it had his attention. His eyes barely flickered as he studied the two images. One was of a woman in a conservative navy suit carrying a briefcase, the other was a long-legged, sultry blonde.

He flipped a page of his own magazine. 'And the camera angle's all wrong.'

Cleo rolled her eyes. *Yeah, right*. 'One way to earn extra money…' She watched him perk up at that, then he narrowed his eyes just enough to provoke her into saying, 'And you'd know all about photographing naked women, wouldn't you?'

'I do not photograph naked women,' he said, stiffly.

'I've seen the evidence, Jack.'

At fourteen it had been too painful and too personal to talk about. Years later it still hurt. She'd barely glimpsed the careless spread of nude photos on the table before his father had swiped them away with apologies on his son's behalf. But not before she'd seen the one including the same woman draped over a formally tuxedoed Jack with a Chesire-cat grin on his face.

'I don't know what you're talking about,' he muttered with a dismissive shrug as he turned the page.

No, he probably didn't even remember—all in a day's work. She directed her attention to the magazine again. 'Cherie here calls it exotic dancing. She says it pays the rent and keeps her flexible.'

He made a guttural sound in his throat. 'If you want flexible, try yoga.'

'I do. I also play basketball and take a weekly jazz ballet class, and it's great, but it doesn't pay the bills. Besides, Jack, I'm sure you've seen your share of "flexible", and I don't think they were performing yoga.'

His jaw kind of clenched but he didn't reply.

Guilty as charged. 'At least she's got a figure, unlike those broomsticks you associate with.' She shrugged at his frown. 'I've seen a picture or two… Somewhere.' The woman draped over his arm in the magazine clipping had been tall, blonde and beautiful. And skinny.

Cleo read on. 'Says here she made enough money to put her through business school. That's how she got where she is today.'

'And where, exactly, is that? With her face splashed all over this magazine, who's going to take her seriously in the workplace?'

'When she's dancing I doubt anyone's looking at her face, Jack.'

Jack made his living out of women who used their bodies in a similar fashion. Even if modelling wasn't stripping, it wasn't far off with today's designs.

'Money's not a problem for you,' Jack said. 'We'll get you settled somewhere and you can—'

'Get…me…settled…somewhere?' She said each word slowly and distinctly between clenched teeth. It took all her self-control to stay seated. 'And if you think money's not a problem for me, you haven't eaten from the plastic spoon I was born with.'

His jaw tightened. 'No, but I've tasted tin a time or two.'

'I make my own decisions. I'm not a kid any more.'

'No. You're not.'

His eyes were focused on her mouth. She could almost feel them sliding over it. Hungrily. She licked her lips. Saw the instant response of his own mouth.

'Which is why I know you'll look at this situation calmly and rationally.' His clipped, dispassionate tone was like a slap in the face. No more hungry eyes. In fact, they looked as dark and remote as a midwinter's night. 'We're going to straighten out a few things while I'm here.'

We? Mr Cool Detached Take Charge Devlin was back with a vengeance. Setting the magazine aside with admirable control under the circumstances, she rose. It gave her a slight advantage in height and some illusion of being in control.

The anger and disappointment simmering in her veins told another story. 'And we have plenty to straighten out. Like I said, I make my own decisions. I'll be looking for a job as soon as possible.' She lifted her chin to stare down her nose at him. 'Perhaps I'll try some of the clubs around town, see if there are any openings for exotic dancers.'

Apart from a tick at the corner of his eye, he didn't react in any way except to say, 'Sit down, you're making a scene.'

Oh. She realised her voice had risen on the last few words and this was Jeanne's place of business, for heaven's sake. For that reason alone, she did as he asked.

But she wasn't finished. His high-and-mighty

attitude needed taking down a peg or two. Leaning over, so she was sure he could see her cleavage, she continued in a lower voice. 'Do you think I'll make a good exotic dancer, Jack?' She toed off her sandal and ran her bare foot under the leg of his jeans, over his shin. And felt him shudder. The hair tickled the sole of her foot, sending ripples up her leg to settle between her thighs.

'Your immaturity's showing,' he muttered, shifting to the left.

'Or pole-dancing,' she continued, undeterred. 'I imagine it's quite...*stimulating*—all that twisting and writhing...' She watched his jaw clench and knew she'd achieved one thing: if she set her mind to it, she could turn him on. Astonishing. However, the operative word here was *if*. 'It's probably quite lucrative. I might look into it.' Satisfied that he was properly *stimulated*, she picked up her magazine and pretended to read.

Thanks to Jack and the mixed signals he was sending her, she was riding an emotional roller coaster. Okay, rule number one: *Keep it light, no one gets hurt.* No way was she going to set herself up for that kind of heartache again.

'Hi, Cleo. And Jack!'

Cleo looked up as Jeanne all but leaped at him. Already standing, he enveloped her in his arms, then kissed her full and firmly on the mouth. A wave of heat plunged through Cleo. He hadn't hugged her like that, hadn't kissed her as if he wanted to eat her alive. So much for light.

That smile, all that devastating Devlin charm, apparently didn't extend to surrogate sisters. He hadn't been on such easy terms with Cleo since she'd been thirteen. She forgot all about keeping it light as a sense of betrayal knifed through her.

'Jeannie,' he said when he came up for air. He stepped back. 'Let's have a look at you.' Jeanne did a quick pirouette, arms outstretched. 'All grown up.' He laughed, low and deep. 'I can hardly believe I'm about to trust little Jeanne with my hair.'

She laughed right back. 'I promise to be gentle with you.'

Cleo knew Jeanne meant nothing by her flirtation, but, feeling as out of place as a chocolate éclair on a platter of prawns, she tapped Jeanne's arm. 'I'll leave you to it, then.'

'Cleo, isn't it great to have him home?' She slung an arm around Cleo's shoulders. 'Are you going to bring him to the game tonight? It'll give me a chance to flirt some more.' She batted her eyelashes at him and grinned.

So much for tonight's idea of escaping his presence for a couple of hours. 'I don't think—'

'I'll be there,' he said.

'Great. Hey, I could maybe rustle up a uniform…'

Cleo's pulse skipped a beat. *Thanks, Jeanne.* She definitely did *not* want to see Jack's tanned, sweat-sheened and muscled body in those ultra-short shorts and loose top. Besides, he was injured.

To her relief he said, 'Not tonight. I think I'll stick to the spectators' stand. My skills on the court are a little rusty.'

Cleo doubted his skills were rusty in any area of his

life, but, after the high-rise stunt he'd pulled earlier, it was a relief to hear him decline.

'Okay, we've sorted out the evening's entertainment.' Jeanne crooked her finger. 'Follow me, Jack.'

'I'll call back in half an hour,' Cleo said, and headed out into the less-unsettling mall.

The strong yeasty smell of hot doughnuts accosted her from the little stand under its pink and white umbrella. For once, her stomach, already tied up in knots, revolted, and she hurried out of the shopping centre into the balmy morning sun.

She walked to the café a few minutes away where the air was fresh and smelled of summer grass and ordered a juice at an outside table. Sparrows darted between patrons, pecking at crumbs. Striped awnings flapped lazily in the drift of warm air.

She leaned back while the waitress set a long, tall glass in front of her.

Why was it so easy between Jeanne and Jack? And why hadn't Jeanne given him the cold-shoulder treatment? Jeanne knew the hurt he'd caused her, even if she didn't know the full story—Cleo wasn't about to let anyone in on that. Was Jeanne taken in by his looks and charm? *Traitor.* It had to be a be-nice-to-the-customer thing.

Even if there was still that rugged, almost primal attraction she doubted any woman under the age of eighty could ignore. The memory of that fast, hard meeting of lips back at the house brought back the giddy rush. Now *there* was a kiss, even if he hadn't meant anything by it. Keeping it light. Except…

She stirred her juice vigorously with the straw and let herself brood. She was going to move out as soon as she could. It wouldn't work at home with Jack there night and day, his scent in the air, that face at the breakfast table, that long, lean body sprawled on the sofa. Not again.

She drummed restless fingers on the table. It wasn't fair that he could simply walk back into her life and turn it upside down. Drag all that old stuff to the surface. Stuff she'd thought she'd buried for good.

His rough-grained voice, the up-for-a-dare attitude they'd shared since childhood. And how, when it had really counted, he'd always, always looked out for her, even if it hadn't been in the way she'd have liked. Even if she'd never admitted it.

Until he'd left.

Her fingers tightened on the glass. *Remember that cold, hard fact.*

She didn't need him looking out for her now. And she certainly didn't want to hear that 'morning after' voice or see those too-clear images it conjured: hot suggestions, hotter bodies…

She rolled the glass against her brow to cool those rampaging thoughts. 'Get over it,' she said aloud. She'd done it before, she could do it again. It was just a matter of will-power.

CHAPTER FOUR

CLEO swiped at her brow, then braced her hands on her thighs as Scott slam-dunked the ball for another two points. The smell of stale sweat and rubber filled the four-court gym. Umpires' whistles, shouts of players and spectators ricocheted off the walls.

So what if she'd heard Jack talking on the phone in the study just before they'd left? In smooth, sexy Italian. She understood the words, *'Ciao, bella.'* And if she'd gotten to the phone first, she'd have known more.

She jogged down the court as Scott dribbled the ball towards the scoring end. Every time she glanced Jack's way he was watching. She ordered herself to concentrate on the game, to ignore the way those dark eyes focused wholly on her. *Will-power, remember.*

But with his hair cut close to his head he looked more like the Jack she remembered and it did strange things to her tummy despite her good intentions.

'Cleo!' Jeanne's shout came too late.

Cleo fumbled for the ball as a blur of brown whizzed past her shoulder. Bugger.

The umpire's whistle sounded. 'Sub. Forty-two out, thirteen on,' their coach, Mike, called, jerking his thumb at Cleo.

Disgusted and worse, humiliated—thanks to Jack—she headed for the bench.

'Your game's off tonight,' Mike said as she grabbed her water and sat down beside him.

'Mmm.' She scowled as her eyes connected with Jack's and felt that stab of heat before she returned her resolute gaze courtside. 'Blame it on hormones.' She yanked the lid off her water bottle.

'Ah.' Mike nodded in understanding.

He didn't understand at all but it let her off the hook.

They won, thanks to Scott's three-pointer on the bell. As the players dispersed Jack joined Jeanne and Cleo as they collected their gear.

'Hey, Jack, still got what it takes?' Scott called, jogging towards them.

Too late Cleo saw the ball leave Scott's grasp. She shot forward to intercept the throw, but it hit Jack high in the chest. She winced as she watched Jack stagger backwards. 'Scott, he's—'

'Fine,' Jack wheezed. But colour leached from his face. He shot a quelling look at Cleo. 'Out of practice.'

He retrieved the ball, tossed it back to Scott, but he didn't fool Cleo. Beneath the grin, she saw the pain the others didn't—Scott was too busy exchanging a male bonding slap with another player and Jeanne was guzzling water.

Turning her back on Jeanne, she glared at him. 'Go ahead, be a superhero,' she muttered.

Jack merely grinned again. 'Give it a couple of weeks.'

'We'll be waiting,' Scott said, turning to stuff gear into his gym bag. 'Okay, one family-size pizza coming up, I'm starved.'

The steamy air carried the odour of hot asphalt and exhaust fumes as they walked across the car park. With what appeared to be some fancy manoeuvring on Jeanne's part, she took the front seat with Scott, leaving Cleo to sit with Jack.

'How do you like Jack's hair?' Jeanne said, buckling her seat belt.

'Good job,' Cleo replied, looking straight ahead. She'd already seen more than she needed to have her fingers tingling at the thought of running them through those gleaming dark strands, touching that bare neck.

'Better than good.' Jeanne turned to grin at them—correction: Jack. 'He looks movie-star gorgeous.'

Scott reversed out of the parking bay, glancing in the rear-vision mirror. 'Our old Jack's back.'

Almost against her will, Cleo slid Jack a sideways glance. He might look more like her old Jack, but for the second time in as many days she reminded herself that looks were deceiving. Behind that movie-star bone structure, under that dark wash-faded T-shirt…

She narrowed her eyes at the darker stain that had spread near his shoulder. Forgot all about keeping her distance and leaned closer. Musky male sweat met her nostrils…and the faint metallic scent of fresh blood.

In the car's semi-darkness she could see the perspiration glistening on his upper lip, the tight muscles in his jaw, the hands clenched into fists on his thighs, but when she opened her mouth his eyes flashed a warning.

'Scott, I think I'll pass on the meal,' she said. Her eyes flicked to the rear mirror and Scott's frown, then back. 'I'm all pizzaed out, and after the stress of yesterday… I'm feeling a little nauseous. Nothing an early night won't cure.'

'Okay,' said Scott. 'You want Jeanne to—'

'Jack'll keep me company…' she lowered her brows at him '…won't you, Jack?'

Scott glanced at Cleo in the mirror again. 'I thought Jack and I might—'

Jeanne's quick not-so-discreet jab cut him off. 'Jack's not the best either, Scott. Can't you see that?' Jeanne shot Cleo a knowing look, a smile hovering around her mouth. 'Men. They never notice.'

Jack made an almost inaudible rumbling sound in his throat.

Cleo sighed. Now wasn't the time to set Jeanne straight. She wasn't sure whom she was madder at, so she settled for as far away from Jack as space allowed, let her head fall back and closed her eyes.

Five minutes later she made a show of dragging herself up the steps to the front door. Bad move, because suddenly Jack was at her side, his palm warm and firm on her basketball singlet, searing her skin and making her jump.

The instant Scott's car disappeared down the drive she jerked away. 'Stop it.'

Undaunted, Jack closed the space again. 'You did this for me.' His breath caressed the side of her face.

The scent of blood and sweat was closer now. 'You're not sick. You go till you drop.'

'And so will you in a minute. Too stubborn to admit when you need help. Well tonight, like it or not, you're going to get it.'

'I can tend my own flesh.'

'Jack. You don't come with me and let me see, I'm going to drag out the old truth-or-dare, and, trust me, you wouldn't like the questions. Take your pick.'

Her heart was pumping in anticipation, but she marched to the kitchen flicking on lights as she went. The first-aid box was in the cupboard above the sink. 'Sit down,' she ordered without turning. Easier to keep her mind off that hot body if she concentrated on what she needed.

She heard the scrape of wood over tile as she set the box on the sink and her heart skipped a beat as she fumbled for a gauze pad and tape.

'When did you develop this bossy, take-charge attitude?' he grumbled.

'Since I took charge when your dad got sick. Take off your T-shirt.'

'I don't need a nursemaid, just give me the box.'

'Save the heroics for someone who cares.' She squirted antiseptic into a bowl of tepid water. 'I know you too, Jack Devlin. Never did want a nurse even when I wanted to play.' She set the bowl on the table. 'Well, I'm going to get my turn now. And it's probably going to hurt...'

Oh, boy. Her breath backed up in her lungs. He'd gotten rid of the T-shirt. Naked skin. Man skin.

Gleaming rich bronze, like polished wood. Heat rolled off him in waves that seemed to soak into her own skin, making her feel hot and shivery at the same time.

'I get the impression you're going to enjoy this.'

His voice held a hint of a smile, and she dragged her eyes to his. There was humour there, and warmth, and for a few seconds she basked in the glory before the ugly sight of his wounds took precedence.

Bruising marred the gorgeous skin, and beneath the shoulder bandage she saw the bright seep of fresh blood. Patches had dried and stuck nastily to his flesh and she winced. 'Ouch.'

'Cleo?' The sharp edge to his voice broke her concentration. 'You sure you're up to this?'

No, she wasn't sure at all, but not for the reasons he thought. The sight of blood didn't distress her; the fact that this was Jack's blood, on Jack's chest, did.

She shrugged to hide her distress. 'What's the big deal?' Biting her lip, she eased away the blood-stiff dressing, and felt him tense when her fingers skimmed over his skin. 'Sorry.'

He hissed out a breath between his teeth, then grinned. Sort of. 'There's a fine line between pleasure and pain.'

'Is that so?' she murmured, chewing her bottom lip some more as she tugged the last corner of the pad from his flesh.

Her breath stalled; she couldn't seem to drag her eyes away from the small, neatly stitched wound and surrounding bruise. 'Is…that…what…I…think…it…is?'

He looked down at the wound then up at her. 'Depends. What do you think it is?'

'You were *shot*?' Her whole body went weak. A ball of ice formed in her chest. A little lower, further to the right, he'd never have come home. She glared at him. 'And what the hell were you doing to get yourself shot?' she snapped, her voice rising a notch. 'A jealous husband?' She raised her hand. 'Don't tell me, I don't want to know.'

She busied herself by cleaning off the dried blood with a cloth dipped in antiseptic. 'It seems to have stopped bleeding.' Her clipped voice betrayed none of the emotions running through her at the thought of losing him for ever.

Yet hadn't she accepted that until yesterday? She shook her head. Not this way. Not dead.

She unsealed a sterile patch, cut two lengths of adhesive tape. 'This'll have to do.' His breath was warm on her hand as she worked. 'It should do the job. For now.'

'Cleo, look at me.' He tilted her chin up until her eyes met his. There were tiny flecks of gold in his irises. She'd never noticed that before. Then again, she'd never been this close, this intimate, for this long, before. 'No jealous husband.'

'Caught between two lovers?' Why was she taunting him? She'd already told him she didn't want to hear.

'You've always had a poor opinion of me,' he said tersely. 'I have not, nor do I intend, to juggle two women at once.' He pinched her chin before dropping his hand, and his eyes hardened. 'One's more than enough.'

She stepped back, heart pounding, mouth dry as jealousy stabbed at her. Who was she—The One that was enough for Jack Devlin? 'Whatever you say.' She busied her hands and eyes repacking the first aid box. 'Go put a clean shirt on; I'll soak this one.'

'Forget the shirt, and the box.' His hand shot out and grabbed her wrist. Hard. She could feel the tension in his fingers, could hear it in his voice, and knew she'd see it in his eyes, but she didn't look.

Instead she stared at her hands, small and fragile-looking against his work-rough ones. Surprising for a photographer, she thought, in some faraway part of her mind.

'You know what really ticks me off?' He said it quietly but Cleo heard the ice-tipped steel lance through it. 'When people closest to me don't accept what I say, don't accept *me*. Dad never did and that's the…' Abruptly he snapped his jaw shut, released her wrist. She saw the shattered look in his eyes before he turned away.

Perhaps he had cared about his father, but something had happened between them that had hurt Jack deeply. Whatever it was he didn't want to show it. Nor did he want to discuss it.

Bright, shiny grief twisted inside her. *I want to accept you. You don't know how much.* Instinctively she stepped back, away from his height and the proximity of that naked chest with its badges of pain.

Through a haze that verged on tears she watched him ball the cloth and walk to the door, the movement as tight and controlled as his face as he turned to look at her for one long, tense moment. And then he was gone.

* * *

The following morning Cleo faced Scott and a stony-faced Jack across a pile of legal documents on the rosewood dining table. She wondered if Jack felt an ounce of the grief that consumed her. It certainly didn't look like it, but she didn't know with Jack any more. Scott didn't look much better; she could have sworn he was nervous.

Scott's jaw tightened, his fingers tense as he shuffled the documents. 'In your absence, Jack, Gerry named you and me co-executors of his will.'

Jack leaned back in his chair as if distancing himself and waved a hand. 'Leave the fine print for now and give us the layman's version, Scotty.'

'He wanted me to read this before the will.' Scott looked at Jack as he unfolded a single handwritten page. '"I have to believe that you, Jack, have taken pity on a dying man, forgiven him and come home."'

Cleo saw Jack's mouth tighten infinitesimally. Enough to know he wasn't as immune to the grief as he'd have her believe. It triggered an echo in her body, a mix of pain and sympathy. She bit her lip and willed herself not to cry. But tears lurked nonetheless.

'Cleo?' Scott leaned across the table and touched her elbow. 'You all right?'

She nodded, thankful it wasn't Jack's hand or she was sure she'd fall apart—from hate, love, anger or grief, she hadn't a clue at this moment.

'Okay.' Scott straightened, eyeing them both in turn. 'Gerry left a substantial estate. Very substantial.' He tabled the documents, then drew a breath. 'Cleo, you are the sole beneficiary of Gerry's will. His bank accounts, stocks and shares, the house and surrounding property.'

Cleo swallowed as her throat closed over. It took a moment to comprehend Scott's words, another to absorb the implications. 'Everything?' Her voice cracked on the word. 'The house and all his money…to me?' She rubbed the heel of her hand over her chest. It felt too tight, too full. *Gerry, how could you do this?* To her. To Jack.

Almost afraid of what she'd see, she lifted her gaze to Gerry's rightful heir. If Jack was disappointed or angry, he didn't show it. In fact, she saw nothing in his dark eyes. And that was the most worrying of all. 'This isn't right, Jack.' She had to work at keeping the tremor out of her voice. 'I know it; you know it.' She pushed the tabled documents firmly towards him. 'It's your family, your inheritance.'

He shook his head. His eyes still gave nothing away. 'Family's not only about blood, as you've demonstrated so well over the past couple of years.' Another man might have sounded bitter. Not Jack. 'It's about caring and compassion and giving. You deserve it.'

Then he flicked the documents as if they were last week's junk mail and the torment she saw beneath that one careless action wrenched at her heart. 'This saves me the hassle of putting the house up for sale. As soon as we've dispensed with the legalities, I'll be gone.'

The cold simplicity of his words slid like ice through her veins. Cleo twisted her hands together beneath the table. If he left mad, hurt, humiliated, it would never be right between them. She had to do something, but what? Nothing could alter the fact that his father had left his inheritance to her.

Scott's eyes softened with sympathy for his friend as his fingers slid back and forth over the papers. No wonder the poor guy looked as if he'd rather be somewhere else. 'Jack,' he said. 'Probate could take up to four weeks.'

When Jack exploded out of his chair, Cleo jolted and looked up sharply. His back was rod-stiff as he strode to the window and she had to stop herself from going to him.

She'd wanted him to help her sort out the legal issues his father's death had left, and God knew he owed her for all those years away. When it was finished, she'd told herself she wanted him gone. No reminders, no pain.

But not this way. Never this way.

She pushed up on wobbly legs. 'I can take care of myself, Jack, but I don't want you leaving with this between us.'

When he didn't reply, she dug down for strength and walked up behind him. His scent, familiar, clean and woodsy, surrounded her. She tapped him on an unyielding shoulder. 'I dare you to stay, Jack Devlin.'

Jack winced. He could feel Cleo's eyes like twin lasers on the back of his head. That compact, curvy body lined up behind him. Too close, too hot, too...Cleo. Stay a month? Out of the question. Hell, staying a day was a day too long. 'You win this one, Goldilocks.'

'Win? This isn't about winning, Jack. It's about having the courage to work with me and make it right. Not a dare, then—I'm *asking* you to stay. To help.'

The quiet sincerity in her voice tugged at his heart. A man could be tempted by that voice, by that woman's scent wafting over his shoulder.

But was that all an act? The splinter of thought struck out of nowhere and festered instantly in his mind. Had Cleo known about the will all along? The more Jack thought about it, the more credible it seemed that she and his father had cooked it up between them. Their relationship had changed to more than father-daughter over the past six years, and Jack was the one on the outside.

Fury erupted like molten poison through his veins. He closed his hands into fists and forced himself to turn and look at her. Had his father's cruel hands—the ones that had broken his ribs—stroked that smooth female flesh?

Was Jack the only one here who didn't know?

Jaw tightening at the sight of her innocent-looking face, he fought back the anger, the bitterness. 'Just think, in a matter of weeks you can play lady of the manor.'

Her face paled, those beautiful blue eyes widened. Then they narrowed and her whole body tensed. She drew a breath and said, 'Now wait just a minute. I'm confused.'

He shook his head to clear it, couldn't stop the sneer that curled his lip. 'That makes two of us.'

'You've made it plain all along you didn't want anything to do with Gerry, and now you act as if I tricked him into leaving me the house.'

'Did you?' The words were out before he could censor them.

She reared back as if he'd slapped her. 'You'd even *ask* that?' Her eyes sprang with moisture, but she swiped at her cheeks with the backs of her hands. 'How could you? How dare you? I'll sell the house. You can have the money or I'll give it to charity; either way it doesn't matter. Money's never mattered to me.'

Her anger only fuelled his own. Questions and doubts hammered in his head. His vision greyed and that throb in his skull was back. 'Unfortunately that's not an option at the moment.' And she'd know it. 'If you need to contact me I'll be down the road at the Sunset Motel.'

Swinging away, he made it through the door and managed to point himself in the direction of the stairs.

'Time out, Jack.'

He slowed in the hallway at the sound of Scott's voice but didn't stop. 'Not now.'

He heard Scott slide the dining-room doors shut. 'I'm sorry, Jack,' he said in a low voice. 'It's a tough break, but you have responsibilities. There's documentation to deal with. You need to be here.'

Jack swung to Scott and met his direct gaze head-on. 'You're co-executor, and the lawyer. You'll manage.'

'What about personal effects?' Scott waved a hand, his frown deepening. 'And the study's full of papers that need going through. Are you going to leave all that to Cleo?'

Too full of anger—and, dammit, pride—to stand

still, Jack paced the hall. Not only had his father denied Jack his inheritance, he'd had the gall to rub his nose in it.

He thought of the school he'd been helping to rebuild before he was shot, the new wells they'd begun to sink. Fresh water and education where it was so desperately needed. That money would have helped.

The old man was counting on Jack's own feelings for Cleo to see it through. If someone had squeezed a round of bullets into his heart it wouldn't have hurt more. His father knew how Jack felt about her. And despised him for it, as if it had been some sort of contest.

Why? Dad had done his damnedest to make Jack look bad in her eyes. Jack always suspected the man couldn't face the prospect of not having a female in his life, as if it was a bruise to his male ego. His cancer would have been the perfect trigger to win over Cleo's sympathy. Or more.

As he passed the dining room he saw Cleo through the glass doors. She was still standing by the window, hugging her arms and looking out across the lawn. Her hair caught the light around the edges, creating a halo effect.

His gut cramped. That damn angel again. Even if she'd been his father's lover, he couldn't cut off his feelings for her any more than he could cut off his own arm. That didn't mean he had to stay and torture himself.

'Jack?' Scott asked quietly.

Not ready to commit to anything yet, Jack rammed a fist into his open palm. 'I'll let you know.'

The back door slapped shut behind him as he crossed the neatly manicured lawn to the place he'd always taken his troubles. The old wattle tree. Beneath its branches the air smelled of summer and dry leaves and solitude. He sank to the ground, leaned against the trunk. Drawing up his knees, he let his forearms rest on them and closed his eyes.

Doc Romano had told him it was important to avoid stress during recovery. *Slow deep breaths, muscles loose. Relax.* But his muscles remained clenched despite his best efforts.

The old *dottore* hadn't met Jack's family.

If you could call it a family. One word summed it up. Dysfunctional. And now the man who called himself a father was leaving someone else everything he owned.

He didn't hear Cleo, rather he felt her presence; a stirring of the senses, like an approaching change in the weather. That light mix of jasmine and woman drifted over him. He wanted to capture that fragrance and carry it next to his heart for the rest of his miserable life. His *solitary* miserable life.

'Jack?' She spoke softly, tentatively, as if unsure of his response. He felt her kneel in front of his raised knees. 'This is new,' she began. 'You were always so revved. I could almost believe you're sleeping.'

He let his eyes remain shut and absorbed the velvet sound of her voice.

'So...if you're asleep you won't hear me apologise for what happened back there.'

An apology? From Cleo? Another reminder that she

was no longer a kid but a mature woman. Question was, what was she apologising *for*? He opened his eyes, then wished like hell he hadn't.

Sunshine and sex.

How was a man supposed to avoid stress, let alone think rationally, when the girl of his fantasies was at his knees, her face inches away from his crotch? He would have risen but for the sudden bulge that surged uncomfortably against the tight seam of his jeans and the fact that he didn't think his legs would hold him.

'Honest to God, Jack, I had no idea about the house.'

'Forget the bloody house. It's just a house.'

She leaned nearer. Her strawberry top gaped, giving him a bird's-eye view of soft shadows and curves. Then, by God, she placed those long, slender hands on his knees.

'Not just a house,' she said. 'And I'm *not* going to forget it. We have to talk.'

The pressure of her fingers burned through his jeans, sending hot darts of pleasure—or was it pain?—shooting up his thighs. The thought of those fingers sliding over his bare flesh, inching up… He cleared his throat, patted the ground beside him. 'For God's sake, sit down.'

To his relief she did as he asked for once. Sunlight dappled her skin as she tilted her head and studied him. 'I don't know the man you've become, Jack. But I want to. We're both different people now. Perhaps we could work on something together, get to know each other again.'

'I'll think about it.' If he could get his brain in gear. Right now the only thing his scrambled brain could conjure up involved nothing more than the two of them and a bed. Maybe not even the bed.

She clasped her arms around her own upraised knees. 'I've been a pain in the bum over the years, I admit it. But you weren't exactly Mr Congeniality yourself.'

He almost weakened. The urge to reach out, to open up and tell her all the reasons why, welled inside him. But the past half-hour had changed everything.

Watching him with those wide, slumberous eyes, she waited for him to respond. To deny his lack of congeniality, perhaps? But she was right on; at this point he felt anything but.

Her jaw firmed, her delectable mouth pursed. 'I assume by that surly expression the answer's no?'

'I said I'll think about it. What do you want, a promissory note?' She blinked at him and he felt a stab of guilt. 'Give me a break, Cleo.'

'Give *you* a break?' She straightened and pulled away. There was a steely edge to her voice that warned him she was stronger than he'd ever given her credit for.

'Do you realise what you said inside?' she continued in that razor-edged tone. 'I don't want your father's money and I'll tell you now, Jack, I won't stand for the verbal slurs you cast on him and me. If you want to follow that path, you can just follow it right back to Italy.

'I want you to stay,' she continued, but he heard a thread of silk through the steel. 'At least until probate's finalised.' She hesitated as if weighing her words. 'I need you.'

The images those three words conjured. His erection quivered and strained against his fly, forcing him to shift position. The sultry glide of her flesh against his as she panted those words into his mouth. His lips sliding lower, driving her desperation higher as her panting turned to whimpers…

Scowling into shrubbery, he avoided the hopeful, vulnerable look that had crept into her eyes, which reminded him his imagination was leading him down the path to self-destruction. He let out a long, slow breath. He could be here for four weeks. Twenty-eight long days. Twenty-eight endless, frustrating nights.

'Think about it, Jack,' she said at last, rising abruptly. 'We'll talk later.'

He remained as he was—hard, frowning—watching the sway of her jeans-clad hips as she walked away. Her gold hair showered over creamy bare shoulders. For a moment he was tempted to follow, just to breathe in its scent again.

He twined his fingers around a slim branch and inhaled the fragrance of the grey leaves instead. Then he rammed a fist against the tree trunk. *Don't be an idiot.* How many men had fallen victim to those blue eyes and pouty mouth in his absence? His own father had left her his entire inheritance—didn't that tell him anything?

But his heart wasn't paying attention to his head. The one girl he'd made off limits was the only girl who'd ever slipped beneath that barrier he'd erected around it.

Damned if he wasn't going to get some answers.

CHAPTER FIVE

JACK followed Cleo at a discreet distance. She headed to the shed at the back of the garage—her workshop, he remembered. He watched her take a key from her pocket, unlock the door and disappear inside. Was she going to fire up her soldering iron or celebrate her inheritance in private?

The images invading his brain tore him to shreds. His father and Cleo. He was so preoccupied with the fist clenched round his gut he didn't knock, but walked right in.

The smell of metal and dust met his nostrils. He gazed at the mess. It was like being back in a war zone. Scrap iron and old pipes were stacked against a wall. Bicycle wheels littered the floor at one end, along with half a dozen metal sculptures—works-in-progress, he assumed, because they didn't look like anything he'd ever seen before. A trio of bronze-forged lilies speared out from a metal cylinder.

A goggled Cleo perched on a stool, head bent over a piece of wire, a snipper of some sort in her hand.

She'd pulled on a pair of grey overalls over her clothes. They swamped her small stature and made her look vulnerable. *We'll just see.* He dragged an overturned crate over the concrete floor, positioning it so he could get a good clear look at her expression, and sat down.

'I'm behind in my orders,' she said, without looking up. She reached for a small mallet and began pounding the metal.

He studied her face. 'Some people might wonder why Gerry Devlin left his house and entire life savings to you over his son.'

The rhythmic thuds continued, but her expression barely changed. 'Perhaps they'll think it's because Jack Devlin didn't care enough to come home when it mattered. But no one's going to wonder, because no one's going to know. We're going to sort it out before they do.'

He watched her clever fingers manipulating the wire as the end took on a flattened oval shape. How clever would they be manipulating his flesh? Or his father's? he thought, clenching his teeth. 'You're not blood kin,' he continued. 'You're a young and available woman. People talk.'

He saw her fingers tighten on the mallet, watched her jaw drop, her throat bob as she swallowed. And waited for her next response. One second, two. Three.

With slow, deliberate movements she set the tool down, slid the goggles to the top of her head, and raised her eyes to his. Their blue fire arced across the space between them. No guilt, no guile. Just simple, honest-to-goodness fury.

Right response.

'What *exactly* do you mean by that?' She spoke each word as if she'd snipped it off with her tin shears. Twin spots of colour bloomed on her cheeks, a stark contrast to the pallor of the rest of her stricken face.

Now he saw the pain warring with the anger in her gaze. He had his answer. Relief pumped through him, but he kept his cool, on the outside at least. And made his decision. 'Exactly what it sounds like,' he replied smoothly. 'Another reason for me to stick around. Quell any speculation.'

'That's obscene.' She glared at him for a full five seconds until he had to glance away. 'The people who knew Gerry and who know me would *know* that's obscene, and they're the only people who matter. Everyone else can go jump.' Her fingers clenched the hammer again. 'That includes you. Money's one thing, but what you're sugges...' Her free hand paused halfway to her goggles. '*Another* reason to stick around?'

'I'm staying till everything's finalised.'

A heavy beat of silence. The only acknowledgement was a curt nod. Snapping her goggles in place, she picked up the wire and attacked it with a vengeance.

Jack couldn't move. He'd hurt her, insulted her, compounded her grief. He slid damp palms over his jeans, curled his guilty conscience into fists against his thighs and swallowed the apology he owed her. If he moved so much as an inch closer, if he let slip one iota of his emotions right now, he'd be lost. He'd have that stiff-as-a-post, overall-covered body against his so quick she'd never know what happened.

'I don't need an assistant,' she said, tossing the mallet down and snatching another. 'And if you don't leave in a matter of seconds, I won't be responsible for what I do with this hammer.'

Without looking at her again, he pushed up and made his way into the fresher air outside. His throat was parched, his chest too tight, his skin damp and prickly. He leaned against the shed wall and took a steadying breath before starting slowly back to the house.

Cleo needed her hammer and hot sticky workshop to sweat out her emotions. In his current medical condition how was he going to sweat out his own?

In the family room he stretched out on the familiar brown leather couch, now covered with a buff throw-over and buttercup cushions. When they were younger, he and Cleo had spent time together in this room, watching videos, playing computer games, listening to music.

He punched a cushion, stuck it behind his head. Responsibility wasn't something he'd had to think about for a long time. He wasn't sure how it fitted on his shoulders. But when it came right down to it, the solution was a perfectly simple three-point plan.

Stay for the next few weeks.

Help Scott tie up his father's affairs.

And walk away.

Oh, yeah, simple. As a distraction, he reached for the TV remote on the coffee-table in front of him and channel-surfed till he found the cricket. Australia versus the West Indies.

The next thing Jack was aware of was the phone ringing. By the time he'd got his brain working and his backside off the couch, Cleo had answered it. He glanced at his watch. Two hours had passed.

He almost groaned. Great. She'd have seen him zonked out in front of the TV, a flaw she'd never failed to point out. He crossed the carpet square and rifled through the neatly shelved books for something to read, but found nothing he could put his mind to. Not that he could put his mind to any damn thing.

A sliver of sun slanting through the window reflected on a gilded hand-decorated box tucked against the wall beside a stash of old vinyl LPs.

Curious, he pulled it out and set it on the coffee-table. Couldn't be personal or it wouldn't be here, he decided, and lifted the varnished découpage lid. Inside he found a photo album. Gold lettering spelled 'Twenty-First' across the front. His heart missed a beat and the old yearning kicked in.

He'd hated missing Cleo's entry into adulthood, even though she'd looked entirely adult enough on her sixteenth. On a spur-of-the-moment thing, he'd sent her an anonymous bouquet of roses for her special day; the only contact he'd ever made. Some comfort that now he could see how she'd celebrated it through another photographer's lens.

'You're awake. Oh...'

He looked up to see Cleo's startled eyes glued to the box. At least she seemed to have worked off her mad. 'If it's personal...'

She shook her head. 'I brought it down the night

after Gerry died. It's been in my room since I put it together.' She lifted a shoulder. 'No one's ever seen it.'

'Not even Dad? Why not?'

She folded her hands together at her waist, and he could see the white-knuckled grasp as she twisted them together. Her face was pale, devoid of make-up as she raised her eyes to his. 'I wanted you to be the first.'

Her choice of words sent heat spiralling through his lower body. He clenched his jaw at the disturbing image of her spread beneath him, slender limbs gleaming in the moonlight, silver hair tangled in his fist, her breath warm against his neck.

Of course his mind was playing tricks. Reading something into her words that wasn't there.

Or was it?

Was there something deeper in that clear gaze? They'd always been close, until she'd grown overnight into the leggy teenager he'd barely recognised. Suddenly he hadn't understood her, hadn't understood himself. The brotherly affection had morphed into something much more dangerous. He'd spent more time with his mates and girls his own age and made a heroic effort to treat her like a kid sister, or, worse, as if he were some sort of father-figure.

She seemed to pull herself together and straightened. 'It's not my twenty-first album, Jack. It's yours.'

His. The breath stalled in his lungs. She'd kept a part of him close all these years. In the sudden stillness that enveloped them he swore he heard his heart beating in time with hers.

He shifted, shaking off the too intimate feeling.

'Why would you do that?' he demanded. 'I'd've thought you'd've burned it by now.'

'Don't think I haven't considered it. I naïvely thought you'd come home.'

All this time he'd imagined her relief that he was finally out of her life. He'd made her existence hell: an older brother's duty. And she'd returned the favour in spades. In fact she'd dug the hole and buried him.

Had he misunderstood her hostility towards him? But he remembered the devastation on her face when he'd kissed her that night. Her mouth swollen and trembling, her eyes filled with shocked horror.

'I'm not so naïve now,' she said. She crossed the room to sit beside him. The heat of her thigh burned through his jeans as she leaned closer to lift out the album.

The first page was a full-sized photo of the three of them. Dad, and a starry-eyed young Cleo gazing up at a younger Jack Devlin. A tumult of emotions washed through him. How many times had he wished he could go back to that point in his life and start over?

'He was like you,' Cleo said, looking at his father's face. 'Quick to butt heads.'

'Yeah.' But Jack wasn't thinking about his father. As she turned the pages he found her time after time, looking too much like a woman for her sixteen years, her heavily made-up eyes sparkling, smile radiant.

Smiling at *him*.

How had he missed that? Because he'd been too busy keeping his own libido in check to pay attention. Something else had been going on beneath that don't-give-a-damn attitude. She'd seen something worthwhile in Jack Devlin.

He'd kissed that goodbye when he'd walked away. *For her own good.* She might be all grown up now, but a relationship was still impossible—for different reasons. *Family and commitment.* Her words echoed in his head.

He wasn't ready for either. For those reasons alone, no way would he start something with Cleo he didn't intend to finish. Nor was he sure he didn't carry his father's violent genes. How many fights had he got into protecting Cleo? He'd prefer burning in hell to hurting her.

He squeezed the hand lying on the album. 'It's a fine record, Goldilocks. Thank you.'

'I didn't do it for you,' she replied, her voice cool. She pulled her hand away. 'I did it for me.'

Beneath the album at the bottom of the box he saw a newspaper clipping, birthday cards, and the single yellow rose he'd given her on the night, carefully pressed.

'Photos were all I had left of you,' she said. The anger he might have expected, and would have preferred, dissipated beneath a kind of resigned acceptance as she replaced the album in its box and set it on the table.

'Cleo, there were reasons…' None of which he wanted to share, he realised as soon as the words were out.

Folding her legs beneath her, she slid one elbow along the back of the couch and faced him. 'I'm listening.'

He hesitated. How to answer? She wasn't ready for the truth so soon after the old man's death. He wanted to stand up, shift away, put some space between them because at that moment he didn't trust himself not to take what his father had accused him of taking that night.

Also preferable to the alternative of looking into those expectant eyes while he concocted a half-truth that might or might not satisfy her. He made a vow then and there that she'd never hear the whole truth from his lips.

'After the party, Dad "requested my presence" in the study to discuss...you.' It had been close on dawn, he remembered.

'Oh...' He saw the flush rise up her neck to stain her cheeks. 'He was pretty mad, I know, but he's never once mentioned that...moment on the stairs...'

Jack knew it had looked bad for him. 'I told him it wasn't what it looked like.' Close enough, though. He'd wanted her so bad he'd ached. *...be out of my sight or I won't be responsible for my actions...* The memory of that defiance, that girl-woman who'd rocked his existence, still haunted him.

'Dad was sloshed and angry with it. We argued. He told me if he saw me again it'd be too soon.'

Right before his iron fist had landed Jack on the floor. *Come on, Jack, boy, fight back like a man.* Closed windows and drapes, low voice. No one ever heard Gerry Devlin raise his voice in anger. Jack had been too busy trying to breathe. By the time he'd managed to half crawl, half stagger to the phone and call Scotty for help, his father had been sleeping it off in his room.

Cleo hesitated as if trying to reconcile what Jack

said with the Gerry she knew. Then a brittle laugh shot from her mouth, shattering the sudden stillness. 'Don't give me that. You and I both know it was the booze talking. You could've waited or come back when he'd slept it off—when you'd both slept it off and cooled down. Why didn't you?'

'Trust and respect, Cleo. Dad gave me neither.' Then he lied when he said, 'I packed and caught the first available flight to Sydney.'

'You know something, Jack?' She leaned towards him, her subtle fragrance filling his nose. Her eyes flashed, an electric-blue charge that seemed to sizzle through the air and along his bones. 'There's more to this than you're telling me.'

He'd been right about not wanting to look at her. She was far too perceptive. He had to look away. 'So now you're a psychologist.'

'No, I'm a woman.'

No argument there. He had a sudden insane urge to give in to his temptation. To absorb all that female energy shimmering from her, to taste it on his mouth, to feel it beneath his palms. Instead he smiled with intended cynicism. 'A man doesn't stand a chance against such powerful logic.'

The air cracked as she slapped an open palm on the couch between them. 'There you go, making fun of me, still treating me like I'm only sixteen.'

'You were never *only* sixteen.' And that had been the crux of the problem.

'How would you know? You barely gave me the time of day except to snap and snarl.'

'Doesn't mean I didn't notice you.'

'You *notice* a toothache. What's more, you do something about it.'

'I did do something about it—I removed myself from the source.' And suffered the pain of loss as keenly as a death. 'It wasn't about you,' he said. 'It was about me.' But he saw the same suffering in her eyes.

Without thought he reached out. He could handle her anger, but not her pain. 'I never meant to hurt you.'

Cleo stared at him, her eyes stinging. The gentle pressure of his fingers, warm, rough-textured as they touched hers, did nothing to ease the ache that gnawed at her heart. Nor did the dark, impenetrable eyes, the musky scent of masculine skin. How could an intelligent, female-savvy man be so dense? 'You really don't get it, do you?'

Or was he playing dumb, refusing to acknowledge what a blind man would recognise when she looked at him? Ignoring her because, let's face it, she was no glamour puss. It was too mortifying to contemplate. And if she didn't do something—anything—she'd dissolve in a puddle of frustration or self-pity. She'd sworn she wouldn't let him make a difference this time—with her head. Her heart wouldn't cooperate.

She forced herself to straighten, pushed up off the couch and away from that male warmth and moved to the door.

'What do you want from me?' she heard him growl behind her.

Gathering what little emotional strength she had left, she turned back. Afternoon sun spilled through the window over his shoulders, a burning aura against the dimness of his face. In his black T-shirt he was the dark fantasy of her dreams.

But unlike in her dreams, he didn't smile and hold out his hand. He looked hard and remote, his lips pencil-thin, the groove cutting between his knitted brows deep and shadowed.

'Nothing. Not a thing.' *Nothing you're not prepared to give willingly.* And, desperate not to give any outward sign of her turmoil, she turned away again before he could answer and fled upstairs to his father's old room.

Closing the door to the room she'd become so familiar with over the past couple of years, she leaned back against it. She could still feel the heat of Jack's hand on hers, could still feel that potent gaze on the back of her neck.

A hint of Gerry's Old Spice cologne, which he'd used till the day he died, clung to the fixtures. For a moment time ran backwards and he was there again, on the silk-covered sofa, his gaunt face turned to the window, eyes fixed on the world beyond. Just as she'd watched through her own window as seasons and birthdays had come and gone.

Waiting for Jack.

Pain sliced through her. Tears clogged her throat. Two people whose stubbornness had cost them one of life's most precious moments—that last chance to say goodbye. Jack had to be wrong. Gerry hadn't meant what he'd said about not wanting his only son to come home.

Though the air was balmy, she rubbed suddenly cold arms. She needed work. Hard, physical work would ease some of the frustration that had built up inside her till she felt ready to explode.

Gerry's bathroom. Not that it needed cleaning—she'd scoured the whole house in the last few days—but working with water always smoothed the rough edges of her mood.

An hour and half a bottle of shower scrub later, she peeled off her latex gloves. She smelled of rubber, probably sweat too, as she pushed a damp tendril of hair from her face. The rest was shoved haphazardly into an old scrunchie she'd found in the vanity. Her eyes caught her reflection in the mirrored wall. And didn't she look like something the cat had dragged in? Thank God she was alone.

As she re-entered the bedroom, the absolute stillness, the emptiness, struck her like a physical blow. To compensate, she switched the CD player on low and let the Beatles sing about 'Yesterday'. Then she walked to the window and pushed it up.

A snappy breeze fanned her overheated face and neck. As she lowered herself to the sofa her fingers closed over the lambswool throw-over and she drew its softness to her cheek. 'You're free now. Free from the pain.'

She hadn't cried at his bedside when Gerry Devlin had breathed his last breath though the grief had cut to the bone. Nor at the funeral; he'd wanted a celebration. But now those tears sprang to her eyes and she let them come. They spilled down her face, cooled by the breeze.

Her hiccoughing breath caught at the sound of the door knob turning. She swiped at her damp cheeks. She could picture Jack standing just inside the doorway, one arm propping up the door-frame, those knobbly toes curling into the carpet, dark eyes watching her.

Watching her lose it.

She tightened her grip on the wool and closed her eyes. Ashamed, embarrassed. Frustrated. 'Go away, Jack.' When he didn't answer, she waved a hand behind her. 'Can't you see I'm having a private moment here?'

He switched off the CD, once again filling the room with silence. 'I've been looking all over for you.'

The air stirred, but he wasn't leaving. Now, when she wished him a thousand miles away… Wasn't it like Jack to be contrary? Her attempt to draw breath came out like a snuffle.

She jumped like a rabbit at the touch of his hands on her shoulders. Awareness sharpened as those hands tightened in a brief squeeze. His heat, his scent, the sound of his breathing washed over her. She felt the sofa dip as he sat down behind her.

'I should've been here for you, Goldilocks.'

'Well, you weren't, so get over it. I have.' *And you're such a lousy liar, 'Goldilocks'*.

'You think things will go on for ever the way they are,' he said. 'That people in your life will always be there, then bam! You wake up one day and everything's changed and it's too late to say all those things you wanted to say, share those thoughts, relive the good times.'

She buried the naïve but romantic thought that he'd

wake up one day and realise all those things could belong to them. And where would she be then? In a nursing home, most likely.

His hands slid from her shoulders, down her arms, and locked in front of her so that she was enveloped in the hard warmth of his body. She gazed down at the sinewy forearms with their sprinkle of cinnamon hair over her own and wondered if she was dreaming.

Her head fell back against the soothing pad of his shoulder as if it had been made for that express purpose. For now she needed his simple offer of comfort. 'I never had a father I want to remember,' she said. His fingers tightened again, and she snuggled deeper into the circle of his arms. 'Not the kind who makes time for you, who loves you for nothing more than for who you are. Your father gave me that.'

'I know.'

She felt the subtle change in his posture. So the reason Jack had dubbed her Goldilocks and said it in that derogatory way of his was a kind of payback.

'We both know he drank too much. The woman he loved was gone, his son…' What could she say? Gerry had seemed indifferent to Jack in the early days, which had developed into open dislike over the years. 'You were rude, always out with your mates. Or some girl or other.'

'You weren't much better.'

She knew he was referring to the rough crowd she'd hung around with—to get his attention. Any attention had been better than none. 'I was pretty obnoxious, I admit it.'

'We were a pair, you and I. Your own father didn't give a second thought as to how his actions affected his daughter. And I lost the mother I loved to him.'

Bitterness flavoured his words and she twisted around in his arms to look up at him. And saw an echo of her own bitterness in those eyes for what their parents had done.

'Jack.' In an automatic response she reached out to his face, wanting to give a little back, to show she understood, that she shared the memories, and the pain.

At the first touch her heart leaped. She absorbed the wonder of the warmth of his skin, the soft stubble beneath her fingers. But his eyes reflected the same shadowed mystery that told her he might have allowed this moment of togetherness but he hadn't lowered his guard.

'I lost a parent too.' Wanting to soothe, she traced her fingertips lightly down his cheek to the line of his jaw. She felt it tighten as he sucked in a harsh breath. Something dangerous flashed in his eyes.

The sweet fledgling elation that had swept her up took a dive. He didn't want her. The stinging heat of rejection rushed to her cheeks. The old, familiar brush-off. Jack didn't like being touched. Leastways not by her. Not home-grown Cleo Honeywell, almost-sister. Six years hadn't changed that.

Blinking back tears still lurking behind her eyes, she curled her hand and fisted it against her breasts. 'I swear, Jack, you wouldn't know if your arse was on fire.'

'Cleo—'

'Don't say it.' She punched the space between them. 'I don't want to hear it.' She could have socked him one for the humiliation alone, but right now that jaw looked as ungiving as granite.

'The back door was open…'

The familiar voice had them both turning towards the door. Cleo wasn't sure who sprang up and apart first. 'Scott.' She forced stiff lips into something resembling a smile. 'Hi.'

Scott stood in the doorway, his business shirt unbuttoned at the neck, tie loose. 'Hi.' Jingling his keys, he glanced from Jack to Cleo, back to Jack. 'If this isn't a good time…'

'It's the perfect time,' Cleo said. Hugging her arms. Achy and embarrassed. How much had Scott heard? She was careful not to look at Jack, but she could feel the tidal waves of tension emanating from him.

'Hey, Scotty.' Jack's voice, all husky and deep and not quite steady.

'So…you two got plans for the evening?'

'No,' Cleo shot back. Not with that sensual scene fresh in her mind. She could still feel Jack's skin against her fingers, his scent filled her nose. His rejection was a raw, throbbing wound that needed attention. Alone. 'I'm going to have a bath and pamper myself. No males allowed.'

'Actually, it was Jack I was after,' Scott said. 'You won't mind if I steal him for a few hours?'

Cleo stifled an almost-laugh. She wasn't invited in any case. 'Go ahead, steal away.'

From the corner of her eye she saw Jack hunch his

The Reader Service™ — Here's how it works:

Accepting the free books places you under no obligation to buy anything. You may keep the books and gift and return the despatch note marked 'cancel'. If we do not hear from you, about a month later we'll send you 6 brand new books and invoice you just £2.80* each. That's the complete price - there is no extra charge for postage and packing. You may cancel at any time, otherwise every month we'll send you 6 more books, which you may either purchase or return to us - the choice is yours.

*Terms and prices subject to change without notice.

If this card is missing write to: The Reader Service, PO Box 676, Richmond, TW9 1WU

NO STAMP
NECESSARY
IF POSTED IN
THE U.K. OR N.I.

THE READER SERVICE™
FREE BOOK OFFER
FREEPOST CN81
CROYDON
CR9 3WZ

shoulders, stick his hands in the back pockets of his jeans and heard him say, 'What did you have in mind?'

'Thought it was time you lost the struggling-photographer look and bought yourself some new clothes. It's late-night shopping in the city. We can take a taxi, grab a meal and a few beers after. Like old times.'

Jack nodded. 'Sounds like a plan. I'll get my wallet.'

As soon as Jack left the room Scott said, 'I interrupted something.'

'You interrupted *nothing*. Have a good time.' *Not.* Avoiding his penetrating eyes, she moved to the door.

He touched her shoulder as she slipped past. 'Don't wait up,' he said softly.

'I don't intend to.' She hadn't fooled him—not best buddy Scott, now Jack's best buddy Scott. She'd been passed over for a guy—how much more depressing did it get?

In her book, depressed equated with a long hot bath, a glass of wine, and a mountain of chocolates. And she had plenty of time to wallow in both the mood and the water.

In Cleo's own bathroom, ferns spilled from hanging pots, towels of peach complemented a wall papered with forest green leaves. It was too early to light candles with the sky still bright with twilight. Said who? In defiance of her own rules, she lit five then steeped the water with a blend of rosemary, lavender and geranium essence. She stripped and sank into the fragrant warmth with her fluted glass and bowl of chocolate truffles.

She'd told Jack she'd forgotten him when he'd left. But she'd kept Pandora's little box of hope tucked away deep in her heart. Believed he'd come home one day and tell her he'd missed her and how she'd grown up and what a big mistake he'd made.

Well, he'd come back, hadn't he? But the rest… She'd almost succeeded in telling herself she didn't care, but seeing him again had undone all that hard work.

It was she who'd made the mistake.

She tossed the glass of bubbly down her throat. And now she was tied to this house by love for his father and a duty to abide by his last wishes.

When the water cooled and the chocolates were gone, she dried off and reached for her pink shortie pyjamas. The soft airy cotton was comforting as she slipped it over her skin.

She padded to her bedroom window and pushed it higher. Outside, the humid, cloud-heavy evening had darkened to indigo. She watched the city lights blinking in the distance, breathed in the scent of damp foliage and frangipani, then switched off the light and climbed into bed.

It was only nine-thirty and she knew she'd not sleep. Not with her traitorous imagination straying to that long, hard body that would be warming the sheets a few feet away when he came home. What would it be like, warming her instead? Her body tingled with the imagined heat, a low throbbing began to pulse in her lower abdomen. She shoved the cover down with an angry sigh. A *frustrated*, angry sigh.

If he came home. With two unattached, attractive men out on the town, she had to face the possibility he might not come home till morning.

CHAPTER SIX

'I WALKED in on something back there.' Scott settled back in the cab, a genuine concern etching his brow and an obvious readiness to listen.

Jack turned to the view beyond the window. He didn't want to discuss it. 'Family politics—a difference in perceptions,' he muttered. Storm clouds were smudging the crimson glow over the city skyline. Inside, the cab's air-conditioning cooled his face if not his body. Somehow Cleo had slipped under his guard.

He'd intended leaving her alone, *should* have left her alone. But he'd had to go find her, hadn't he? After all, he'd laid some heavy-duty information on her this afternoon. But those few moments on Dad's sofa hadn't been about his father so much as comfort. It had nearly cost him his hard-earned self-control. Jeez, if Scott hadn't turned up…

He shifted, suddenly uncomfortable as a surge of remembered heat swamped him.

'I take it you mean your father?' Scott asked quietly.

Jack nodded. 'He meant a lot to her. I can't just hit

her with the truth. I don't think she could deal with it. Nor should she have to,' he finished harshly.

Scott squinted into the sun setting below the band of clouds and the silhouettes of Melbourne's approaching skyscrapers then turned to him. 'What are your plans for…after?'

'You mean after probate's granted? I've unfinished business overseas.' Nothing had changed. His job as a photographer was still open; he could resume it if he chose. Or he could return to the town he'd been helping rebuild before he'd been shot.

'Unfinished business,' Scott repeated, breaking into his thoughts. 'Anyone special we should know about?'

Anyone special. Cleo's scent still clouded his mind, the imprint of her hands were still fresh on his face. Needing a distraction, Jack inched the window down a fraction. Air laden with exhaust fumes and hot bitumen rushed past his ears. He laughed without humour. 'You know me—too many to count.'

'I do know you, Jack, perhaps better than you know yourself. If you get close and personal with Cleo then skip out on her, she's going to hurt.'

'I haven't laid a finger on her.' Yet. 'That's why I want this over. She doesn't need me screwing up her life.' He shrugged at Scott's intense scrutiny. 'I'm surprised she's not already attached. She must have men in her life. You, for instance.' And as much as it pained him, if Cleo and Scott had something going, at least Jack could rest almost easy knowing she'd be okay.

'Me?' Scott shook his head. 'She doesn't look at me

that way.' He cocked a brow. 'But she looks at you. She's always looked at you.'

A strange but powerful sensation steam-rolled through Jack, leaving him feeling bruised and breathless. He'd seen it today, in the photos, on the sofa—a woman's eyes, a woman's desire. But no matter how much he yearned to fill the empty space inside that he'd always held for her—only her—he must discourage any feelings she had for him. He covered his regret with a dismissive gesture. 'I'm never in one place long enough, Scotty, you know that. Cleo wants a home and family. She deserves it. But after what I went through as a kid, family life's not for me.'

'Give it time, Jack.'

He smothered the sigh that came from his heart. 'I won't be here long enough.'

Jack was still brooding about that two hours later as he drew wet circles on the buffed wood-grained table with his moisture-slick glass of beer. His fourth, or was it his fifth? He shrugged, took another gulp. Its yeasty taste slid down his throat. Who the hell cared? If he wanted to get plastered, that was his business.

Laser lights swirled, bass thumped. The music was hot, the entertainment hotter. His eyes might be directed at the dance floor but his mind was fixed on the distressed woman he'd left in the hallway.

He shouldn't be staying in that big old house alone with Cleo. Yet he had no choice with his father's mess to tidy up.

She'd *looked* at him. And he'd felt the intensity all the way to his soul. Even half-crazed with jealousy and liquor, it hadn't been disgust he thought he'd seen in her eyes that night six years ago—she'd wanted him. And he'd hurt her. Even then she'd not given up on him.

She should have.

It would only lead to heartbreak. He wasn't ready to settle down, and if he ever was it wouldn't be in that house, with those memories.

'Scotty, go get us a couple of shots of Jack Daniels each, would you?'

While Scott fought his way to the overcrowded bar, Jack scowled some more while the action played on around him.

'Admiring the talent?' Scott said, setting the drinks in front of Jack.

He poured a shot of the potent liquid down his throat.

Scott laid a hand on Jack's shoulder. 'You're going to hate yourself in the morning.'

'Might as well make it worthwhile.'

'Time to go, pal.'

He pushed out of his chair, slung an arm round his mate's neck. 'Let's go home.'

Scott steered him towards the exit. 'We'll swing by my office on the way and pick up your shopping. Perhaps you'll have sobered up some by the time we get there.'

Jack wasn't sure how many drinks he'd consumed but it annoyed the heck out of him that Scott was still ostensibly sober when they arrived home. He'd always been able to drink Scotty under the table. A side-effect of surgery? He patted his dressing; at least the booze had dulled the ache in his shoulder, if nowhere else.

The house loomed ahead in the sweep of headlights. What the hell time was it? Apart from the security light that winked on as the taxi approached, the house was in darkness.

He hauled himself out, and, swaying a little, stared up at the second storey windows. One in particular. The warm evening breeze stirred the leaves and caressed his face. The way Cleo had caressed his cheek this afternoon.

She must be in bed. He imagined that compact little body warming the sheets, hair spread like a golden fan, and fantasised a moment about what she'd be wearing. Silk, lace, cotton? Or nothing at all.

His whole body went tight as a bow string. Did she sprawl, those slender, creamy arms and legs tangling with the linen, or did she like to curl up? He wished he didn't want to know.

He dug in his pocket for his keys as he made his winding way up the path. No stars tonight. Thunder rumbled in the distance. The air was thick and still.

'Jack, wait up.'

He turned, noticed his legs wobble, and squinted at Scott striding towards him with an armload of shopping bags. 'Thanks.' He took the bags, and, full of good cheer, gave him a hug. 'You're an okay guy.' Then he gazed up at her window again. 'Beam me up, Scotty.'

Scott's eyes followed. 'Not a good idea, my intoxicated friend.'

'I guess you're right.'

'I know I'm right. Can you make it upstairs yourself? The traditional way?'

'Sure. Just like old times, eh?'

'You got it.'

'Later.' Jack raised a hand in farewell as he leaned against the verandah's stone pillar and watched Scott climb into the cab and disappear down the drive and into the night. Yep, just like old times.

Except... This afternoon everything had changed. Jack sucked in a lungful of the heat-drenched evening to clear the alcohol-induced haze. The one thing that hadn't changed was how he felt about Cleo. Always that gut-churning, heart-grabbing reaction, an ache so familiar it had become a part of him. He fumbled the key in the lock.

And seeing her again...the instinctive urge to reach out and touch that petal-soft skin, to drag her against him and bury his nose in all that fragrant hair, hadn't faded.

It had just grown stronger.

He heard a rustle in the bushes as he opened the door. 'Evening, Cont...Constantine,' he managed around a rubber tongue. 'An evening out with the ladies?'

Con prowled over and wound his way once around Jack's legs before shooting inside. Jack thumbed on the hall light to see his way upstairs and followed the huge furry shape. Con stopped at Cleo's room, flicked his tail, obviously irritated to find the door shut.

'You and me both,' Jack muttered. She must have

taken a shower—he could smell the fresh scent on the air mixed with the familiar smells of polish and wood.

The light in the stairwell threw long shadows down the hall. He was inebriated enough to consider opening her door and finding out if his fantasy about her preferred sleeping position was true, but—sadly—not inebriated enough to carry through. So he stood a moment breathing in her fragrance while Con sat watching the door, his mismatched eyes expectant.

'If I can't, you can't,' he told Con. No way was he going to open that door, even for a cat. Especially not for a cat. Royally ticked off, Con rose and stalked on down the hall, tail bristling.

'Okay, time for bed.' The floorboard creaked beneath him. Leaning against the wall, he toed off his shoes. 'Sh. Mustn't wake Cle...'

The almost inaudible click of the door froze him in place. The door opened and a cloud of tousled hair glinted in the light, then an elegant bare shoulder.

Holding his breath, he watched from behind while thousands of forbidden thoughts played through his mind, all of which involved that bare flesh. Starting with sliding his hand under that skinny strap and easing it down...

'Bastard,' he heard her mutter quietly. Then she turned his way.

She wore a tiny pair of pale panties that flared at the hem, exposing the tops of her smooth, creamy legs, and a matching top that stretched over her breasts like opaque cling-wrap. In the soft yellow light the colour blended with her skin, making her appear naked. God help him.

Her hand flew to her throat. 'Jack! What are you doing here?' She didn't look pleased to see him.

He thought he felt a grin spread over his face. Or a grimace. 'Loitering?' When she simply gaped at him, he straightened—or tried to. 'Chain me to your bed. Make me confess, I—'

'Shut up, Jack,' she said, between clenched teeth. 'If you have to bring your playmates here, at least have the decency to keep it discreet.'

He frowned. 'Say what?'

'The woman you brought home with you.' She glanced up and down the hallway. 'The one you were talking to.'

'The one I…uh…Con. I was talking to Con.' Perhaps that was why his tongue felt thick and furry.

On cue, the fluffy feline padded out of Jack's room towards them.

'Oh.' She flushed and lowered her head. 'There you are, you naughty boy,' she said as Con disappeared into her room. She raised her eyes to Jack's. 'I apologise… I shouldn't have jumped all over you like that…'

All over you. 'Like honey over hot fudge.'

'What?'

Had he lost control of that thick, furry tongue too? 'Nothing. No need to apologise, s'okay.' He took a step, tripped on his own damn shoes that he'd forgotten he'd removed. Uh-oh. Fighting inevitability, he stumbled forward, trapping her against the wall.

Her breasts collided with his chest. Her eyes flew to his, wide and almost green in the light. He could see the pretty pulse beating fast against her throat, matching his.

His hands had connected with her shoulders. He wanted to slide them down her arms, to feel that warm, silky skin and the firm muscles beneath, to watch her eyes widen with awareness while he did, but opted for the wall on either side of her head.

He should step away now, go to his room, but it was as if he were encased in stone. He sucked in air, immersing himself in the fragrance. 'You smell like a garden.'

'Can't say the same for you; you smell like a brewery.' Her breath whispered over his skin. His gaze dropped to her full, sensuous lips, slightly parted. She remained as she was as if waiting.

Thunder rolled across the sky. Through the open window in her room a layer of humidity swamped them, making her skin dewy and slick.

She moved oh-so-subtly, so that he felt her nipples rise like two little beads against his shirt. And felt the hot, liquid slide towards total meltdown. Sweat broke out on his brow; his arms were beginning to tremble. Her mouth was a whisper away. He was hard and hot and only human.

That first contact was like laying his lips on a live wire. The sensation sizzled along nerve endings and spun through his head. He tangled his hands in her hair as he'd always imagined doing, let the silky strands caress his fingers, and shifted nearer.

In response, she moved her hips lightly against him, a soft noise coming from her throat, like a purr. He felt her mouth soften and give and took instant advantage, plunging deep, dancing his tongue over hers.

He'd known how she'd taste without the bitterness of anger. Exquisite. Sweet, dark and rich, like the imported cherry liqueur his father kept for special occasions.

Coming home.

This was what he'd wanted all these years. What he'd never found with any other woman. This connection, this rightness.

Then he couldn't think, didn't want to analyse. His thumbs moved to her face, exploring the satin softness of the skin beneath her jaw, her neck, the little hollow above her collar-bone where her pulse jittered.

He felt her arms slide around his waist, the heat of her hands burning a trail up his spine as she stroked him. She shifted, arching towards him.

Wanting more, he slid his own hands lower, over soft cotton and feminine curves. His thumbs whisked over taut nipples beneath the cling of fabric. With something close to reverence he filled his palms with the firm but luscious weight of her breasts.

Her quick intake of breath, the moan from her throat, brought him up and out of the grip of his sensual haze. What in hell was he doing? Clutching for some shred of sanity, he jerked himself away. His lungs burned, his lips were on fire. And his rock-hard erection throbbed like a wound.

She blinked at the sudden movement, those thick gold lashes sweeping her cheeks, then stared up at him, eyes glazed. Something dark and passionate simmered in their depths, and something more: shock.

And no wonder. The scene was like an old movie

rerun. Except that this time he'd not stopped at a kiss; he'd groped her like a randy teenager. His drink-hazed mind rejected the knowledge that she'd done her own groping.

Cleo. The kid who'd smeared jam on his bike when she'd been too young to ride with him, the one whose knee he'd tended when she'd sneaked out to road test that same bike.

The girl who'd always been there, in his life, in his thoughts. The girl he'd never been able to touch.

And he still couldn't touch her because he'd made a promise to himself.

Because they were shaking, he lowered his hands, forced them into fists at his sides. Took a step away. Futile to hope she hadn't felt his arousal.

She wouldn't know it went so much deeper than sex—after all, he'd done it before with much the same result. Pain clawed viciously around his heart. 'I'm sorry.'

Pathetic. He wasn't sorry. Already he wanted to do it again.

Her eyes widened and the limpid pools hardened to glacial ice. The mouth that he'd all but devoured thinned. Then one hand shot up and he felt the sharp sting of her palm against his cheek.

The slap echoed like a gunshot in the muggy stillness. Then she hugged her shoulders as she backed towards her bedroom doorway. Her eyes glittered with unshed tears; her lips still glistening from their kiss, trembled.

'Cleo…'

She flapped a hand and he had to stop himself from reaching for her. 'Just so you know,' she said, her voice husky, breaking. 'That's for the apology.'

Before he could get his head around her words the door slammed shut, rattling the trio of watercolours on the wall.

He stood watching it a moment, rubbing the hot, stinging spot on his cheek. The *apology*?

He'd changed their relationship yet again. One thing hadn't changed: his feelings towards her. But now, whenever he looked at those lips, he'd remember how they'd felt in the bloom of passion.

And want it again.

Scott was right. Jack Devlin was going to hate himself in the morning.

Cleo sagged against her door. She barely registered the flash of lightning through the window. Barely noticed the first big drops of rain plopping on the leaves outside.

Her whole body felt as if it were on a knife's edge. Weak, helpless, burning… She lifted trembling fingers to her mouth and a whimper escaped. Oh, she burned all right, from the tingling in her still kiss-sensitive lips to the wave of liquid heat low in her belly, to the soles of her bare feet.

He'd wanted her. He'd wanted her as a man wanted a woman. She'd seen it in his eyes, smouldering and ready to ignite. She'd felt it in his unsteady breathing, the way he'd tensed his muscles as he'd leaned into her.

And most telling of all: he'd been big and hard and

all male. She might not be too familiar with male arousal, but she'd known exactly what she'd felt nudging her belly. She shivered at the thought of that impatient masculine part of him sliding inside her.

And the memory of his hot, restless hands cupping her—her breasts felt full and heavy beneath her pyjama top. Her nipples, still tight and erect, prickled.

Her jaw tightened. The impact of what he'd done seeped through the heat haze and her anger resurfaced. He'd *apologised*. He'd denied what they had, denied both of them.

He'd lifted that lid on her Pandora's box, shown her the delights inside, then slammed it shut. And apologised.

How dare he? The jerk. Was he sorry because he was drunk or because he'd kissed her?

She hadn't waited to find out. She'd had control over that small action at least. But the rest… Her breath whooshed out. Unable to think beyond the moment, she'd been all but molten metal in his hands, letting him mould her to his will with his clever fingers, his mouth, his body…

She needed to lie down.

Her legs felt weak as she crossed to the bed. The inside of her thighs felt chafed, sensitised from the rough weave of Jack's trousers.

Con swatted an impatient paw when she pushed at him, and stalked to the foot of the bed—typical male, wanting it all his way.

Punching the pillow, she flopped backwards and lay in the murky evening-scented stillness, gazed at the ceiling. 'I've got news for you, Jack. Tomorrow you pay.'

CHAPTER SEVEN

CLEO was awake with the dawn's first streaks of crimson and gold. The night's storm had blown away, leaving the clear blue sky of another hot day. Thanks to Jack she'd tossed all night, but she rolled out of bed with a plan.

She hadn't discussed the mutual project idea she'd come up with yesterday but the sundial and memorial garden she'd intended creating was something they could work on together.

Dragging on her gardening shorts and jersey top, she rooted in her closet for her old sneakers. Something to focus on might ease the awkwardness she knew she'd feel when she saw him again.

All Jack's fault. And what did she have to feel awkward about? She paused in her task of tying her laces. But, ooh, could the man kiss when he put his mind—and lips—to the task. No wonder he had females lined up. He could make a woman feel as if she were the only one in the world. A dangerous skill, she decided, glaring up the hallway at his closed door before descending the stairs to the kitchen.

She fed Con, then grabbed a peach. As she bit into the fruit she tried not to imagine the same body that had plastered her against the wall last night sprawled on the bed upstairs. Reckless thoughts like that could sway her from her intention to make him pay this morning. She hoped he felt like hell when he woke. Apology *not* accepted.

She grabbed a mug and herbal tea bag, slammed both on the counter and poured boiling water over, nearly splashing herself in the process. Would he agree to her idea?

She shrugged it away. What was not to agree? He had nothing but time on his hands. Might as well put those hands to good use. Her nipples sprang to attention when she remembered the use he'd put those hands to last night.

Clenching her teeth against the traitorous tingle, she twisted her hair into a knot, shoved it under an old baseball cap and let herself out into the fresh morning air.

She was *not* going to think about it. He probably wouldn't turn a hair when he saw her again.

She needed to maintain an it-happens-all-the-time façade. So she would not let him see how embarrassingly inexperienced she was. She'd managed to carry it off at sixteen; she could do it now. He didn't need to know that, apart from one not-so-memorable night months after Jack had gone, she'd not let any guy past first base.

She headed for the gardening shed, anxious to get a head start before the day grew hot. The door opened with a scrape of wood on stone, and a musty, earthy smell met her nose. Selecting tools, she dumped them in the wheelbarrow.

The spot she'd chosen for the garden was in the centre of the front lawn. Using stakes and twine, she marked out a circle, then dug a groove with the tip of the spade.

She leaned on her spade and swiped at her brow. She'd made the sundial and gnomon using scrap metal and an old piece of iron lace she'd salvaged at a demolition site. She would ask Jack to help select the flowers, and, if his shoulder was up to it, he could plant them. That way, they both had a hand in creating a lasting memory.

But his injury had her thinking again. What had he been involved in to get himself shot? She'd have to pry it from him the way she tackled her metalwork—slowly and sensitively.

But slow and sensitive wasn't the way she intended waking him this morning. She checked her watch as she headed for the house, mentally rubbing her hands at the prospect of rousting him out of bed and seeing him suffer the effects of his overindulgence. Or his underperformance?

Squeezing her eyes shut, she mentally counted to ten. In Chinese. She was thinking about it again. The thing she wasn't going to think about. The lip-smacking, hip-grinding thing. If they were going to complete this project, she was going to have to stay cool—a problem if Jack was going to look at her the way he'd looked at her last night. That hot, hungry way.

Last night had not been the act of a man in control. A man recovering from God knew what—he hadn't let her in on his past. A past he was going back to. Didn't that tell her anything? He didn't want to be a part of her life.

So it suited the mood she'd talked herself into to rap once then push the door open. She stood a moment, letting her eyes adjust to the semi-darkness, trying not to inhale the not-so-subtle smell of stale booze and male sweat.

Jack was flopped on his stomach, one sinewy arm hanging over the bed. The sheet was scrunched at the bottom of the bed. A surge of heated excitement raced through her body, and pooled between her legs. She was right—Jack Devlin slept in nothing but a tan.

The acre of bare bronzed back and the long dimpled spine had her palms itching to touch. But she was powerless to resist following the tight curve of his slightly spread muscular buttocks with its shadowed cleft, to the darker hint of male anatomy between two firm thighs… The moist heat between her legs intensified and her pulse rate soared. The fact that she was viewing something forbidden only added to the mix. Her common decency seemed to have deserted her.

She licked her lips. The urge to trail her tongue over all that taut, hot skin overwhelmed her. And how was she going to keep that emotional distance? She'd never be able to look at him again and not remember.

Finally, reluctantly, she dragged her gaze to his pillow. His mouth was full and gorgeous and relaxed in sleep. She remembered only too well how it had felt against hers, how persuasive that mouth could be.

Scowling, she huffed out a breath, stuck her itchy hands in the back pockets of her shorts and said, 'I knocked.' The dark lashes didn't so much as flicker. 'Wake up, sleeping beauty, time's wasting.'

She moved to the curtains. They slid apart with a swift whoosh. Air that had been trapped behind the drapes wafted fresh and cool through the window and over her skin. Sunlight flooded the room.

'God,' a voice rasped from the bed.

She took some satisfaction at seeing him wince. 'No, just Cleo, I'm afraid, with your not-so-early wake-up call.'

'I didn't order any wake-up call,' he mumbled.

'Rise and shine, we've got work to do.'

He started to roll over, then stopped. 'Hey, I'm naked here.'

'Well, you're conscious, at least. Downstairs, ten minutes, if you want breakfast.'

She flicked the switch on the radio and racked up the volume on a heavy-metal station on her way out. If he swore, she didn't hear.

When he made his appearance twenty minutes later, it didn't look as if he'd be big on conversation this morning. His face was drawn and slightly green, accentuating his stubble, but he'd taken a shower, leaving his hair damp and smelling fresh and spicy. He was wearing long shorts and a ratty T-shirt he must have unearthed from his six-year-old supplies. He walked carefully, as if measuring his steps.

'No breakfast,' he said in a downright pitiful voice as he filled a mug with water at the sink.

'Oh?' When he scowled at her, she pointed to the fridge. 'Tomato juice is good for hangovers.'

'Don't need it,' he growled, zapping the mug in the microwave, then dunking a teabag in.

'Glad to hear it, because we've got work to do.' She pushed up. 'Bring your tea and come with me.'

Moments later they stood on the lawn where Cleo had marked out the circle.

Jack was silent a moment, his expression blank. 'A garden? Or are you planning a pond?' *And what do you need my approval for?* his expression said.

She could almost feel his head pounding as he shaded his eyes from the morning glare. 'A memorial garden with a sundial,' she explained. 'Our mutual project.'

His dark brows lowered, his mouth turned down. Yesterday she might have laid a hand on his shoulder, but this morning was an entirely different matter. Instead, she stuck her hands on her hips. 'You have a better idea?'

'You have to know how to make a sundial,' he said with an arrogant wave of his mug. 'You need to find north, know the latitude, you can't just—'

'Done already.' Annoyed that he assumed she hadn't done her research, she crossed her arms over her breasts. 'All you have to do is help with the garden.'

'Hmmph.' He squinted as he surveyed the circle.

'I know your shoulder's still healing. I can dig—'

'I'm not an invalid.' He rotated his shoulder. The muscles bulged like coiled rope in his forearm as he flexed his hand.

'Good.' He was standing too close. Scowling. Looking dangerously dishevelled, smelling of soap and man. 'I'll get the hose and soften the ground.'

She swung away, intent on putting some distance between them, but he grabbed her arm with one firm hand, tossing his mug on the grass with the other.

'Not so fast.' Strong fingers closed around her wrist. Useless to try to pull away. 'We need to clear the air first.'

She looked up into dark, whiskey-coloured eyes. 'Clear the air?' The air she could feel pulsing thick and charged between them?

'I shouldn't have kissed you like that.'

'Like what?' *Like a man kisses a woman?*

'In that condition. I wasn't at my best when I got home last night.'

'That's too bad.' She couldn't help the inward sigh. How would his best feel? Not that she was going to find out. *Remember the Rule.* Playing it light, she patted his T-shirt, concentrated on its wash-worn softness and tried not to think about the hard chest beneath. Then she grinned and said, 'I wasn't at my best either.'

Something dangerous speared into his eyes. She could almost feel the heat. Her stomach muscles curled. She tried to step away, but his hold was like a steel band. 'Play grown-up games the way you did six years ago and live with the consequences.'

A flush crept up her neck at the memory. 'I'm old enough to play grown-ups now, Jack. And have been for some time.' She meant *old enough*, but by Jack's glowering expression he was stuck on the *playing grown-ups* bit.

His jaw clenched, and his grip on her wrist tightened. 'You want to be real careful about airing your conquests to me, Cleo.' Beneath the holier-than-thou attitude she remembered so well, his eyes smouldered with that same hot spark she'd witnessed last night.

In daylight with the sun catching the red-gold strands in his dark hair, with the sound of birds and breeze, it was no less potent. But she saw something darker flicker in their depths now.

Lord in heaven…could he be jealous? She almost laughed aloud. Jealous of her non-existent love life. But her pulse picked up as the flicker in his eyes intensified to an all out blaze, and a fine tremor shivered through her limbs. 'Women don't make *conquests*,' she retorted, maintaining her calm. 'We're far too evolved.'

'The way you went about it at my twenty-first you could've fooled me.'

Because his rejection had forced her to do something she'd never done before: come on to a guy. 'I've seen you in action too, remember.' Memories she wanted to forget. Snapshots of nudes and Jack, a hidden photo in her drawer she wished she'd never seen.

'That was a long time ago. It's a new day and I'm sober.' He was rubbing a callused thumb lightly over the pulse in her wrist now and watching her with such tenderness, she wanted to sigh.

Suddenly his lips were a whisper away from hers, his breath warm and smelling of tea. Her mouth dried up; her knees went weak. He pulled her closer, dropped her now-limp hand to slide his thumb across her lower lip, leaving tingles of sensation. A hot shiver rippled down her spine. Nearby, a lawnmower droned and the smell of fresh-cut grass lay on the morning air.

'Jack…' She let out a shaky breath as his mouth skimmed a lazy path along her jaw. Coherent thought spiralled away on the breeze. Her eyes drifted closed at the stunning sensation of his lips on her skin. The warmth dancing on her eyelids faded as Jack's head blocked the sun. Anticipation quivered through her.

His lips moved to her neck, he released her arm, leaving both his hands free to caress up and down her spine. The world tilted on its axis and then… No more Jack. She heard a sharp sigh as he stepped back. She let her own sigh out slowly. Raggedly.

'Hell,' he swore softly and turned away.

Her fingers fumbled as she straightened the cap on her head. 'You kissed me last night, Jack. You might have been under the influence, but you wanted me.'

He paced away, dragged a hand over his head, then swung to her. 'Cleo…' There was something horribly, ominously final in that one word. He started back, stopping when he was an arm's length away. She saw his Adam's apple move as he swallowed.

Yes, he wanted her. But he didn't love her. Not the way she wanted him to love her. Could she settle for that?

She'd waited a long time for him to open his eyes and look her way. Tears gathered at the back of her throat. She tugged the bill of her cap down further so that it shaded her eyes. She didn't want to see him, didn't want him seeing her humiliation.

He moved closer, placed impersonal hands on her

shoulders. 'I don't want to start something I can't finish. You mean too much to me, Goldilocks. I'm not a permanent kind of guy; I only came back to finalise Dad's affairs.'

She knew that, she'd always known it.

You mean too much to me.

Desperate not to let him see how much it hurt, she shrugged beneath his hands but they stayed firm and uncompromising, the way his six-foot height towered over her. 'That's right, Jack. Don't let a little lust over a home-town girl get in the way of life's priorities.'

His eyes darkened. 'Don't cheapen what we have, or who you are.'

'What *do* we have?'

Hesitation. A muscle tightened in his jaw. 'I don't know.'

She shoved at his hands and this time he let them fall to his sides. Anger exploded out of her. 'You haven't been paying attention, Jack.'

'Oh, I've been paying attention. You've made it plain that you disapprove of my choices and the way I live my life. I have to think about this…for both of us. That kiss last night—'

'What kiss?' she hurled back. 'And I do my own thinking.' This time it was she who stepped away. 'When I decide what's right—for *me*—I'll let you know.'

'Another day with no one but Jocular Jack for company and I'd've gone crazy.' Cleo faced Jeanne across the café's red-and-white-checked table cloth and stirred her coffee. 'Thank God for you, Jeanne. Our Sunday-morning brunches are a life-saver.'

Jeanne smiled. 'Is Jack giving you a hard time?'

'Try *any* time.'

Jeanne's smile faded. 'Oh.'

'He's been back over a week and I still don't know the real Jack Devlin.'

'Does anyone ever know the real anyone?' Jeanne bit into her apple Danish. 'It's bound to take some adjusting. He's been gone a while.'

'I guess.' Frowning, Cleo lifted her cup to her lips. They'd stuck to their agreement and worked on the sundial thing. They'd dug dirt together, positioned the dial, planted petunias. Talked in monosyllabic sentences.

So much for getting reacquainted.

'I take it your feelings haven't changed,' Jeanne said.

When Cleo could only shake her head, Jeanne reached over and patted her hand. 'Go ahead, let it all out. You're talking to Auntie Jeannie here.'

'It's embarrassing. Humiliating, even.'

'Why, for God's sake?'

'Well…' She swallowed, unsure how or even whether to go on. 'I look at the two of you. You're great together.'

'Of course. He's a friend, but—'

'He hugged you. Kissed you.' *And practically stuck his tongue down your throat.*

Jeanne nodded. 'A natural enough way to greet a friend you haven't seen in six years.'

'He didn't hug *me* like that.' She couldn't help it; her lip curled. 'All spontaneous and smiley.'

'Oh, Cleo, don't be mad at him. Jack and I have always been close.'

'That's just it—you two are so natural and easy with each other.'

'Yes. We're comfortable together. But there are no sparks,' Jeanne said gently. 'We're like brother and sister. Whereas you two… You strike so many sparks off each other, it gives me the hots. You were a kid when he saw you last. Even then I saw the way he looked at you, but he was way too nice a guy to take advantage of your youth and innocence.'

'So what, now I'm old and experienced?' Cleo shook her head. 'And he still hasn't taken advantage of me.' She was older of course, but experienced…hardly. Not when her love life had been on hold since Jack had left.

'He's still getting to know the grown-up version,' Jeanne said, skimming a spoonful of froth off her cappuccino.

Cleo propped her chin on her hands. The memory of just how well he'd been 'getting to know' her passed in front of her eyes. 'He kissed me the other night. Drunk as a skunk, but he kissed me.' And she could still feel the press of that hard male body against hers.

Jeanne leaned forward, spoon poised halfway to her mouth, her expression bright and interested. 'Well…?'

'Then he apologised.'

Jeanne made a sound that was part sympathy, part amusement. 'Poor Jack.'

'Poor *Jack*?'

Jeanne-the-traitor smiled. 'What happened then?'

'Nothing. Oh, I slapped him.' At Jeanne's incredulous expression, Cleo waved her hand. 'For the apology. We talked around it a bit the next day. We argued. No more kissing, no more talking. Said he wants to think about it for both of us. Like I've got no say in the matter.' Anger prickled her skin just remembering it. 'Can you beat that?'

'I can't, but you can.'

'Me?'

'Yes, you.' Jeanne fixed Cleo with a straight look. 'Nothing's stopping you taking the initiative, is it?'

Cleo frowned, considering the notion. 'I guess not.'

But could Cleo Honeywell the homebody really measure up to Jack's ideal of a desirable woman? Did she want to know? Could she live with the answer? Only one way to find out.

Jeanne's nail tapping on the table cut into her thoughts. 'If you want him, do something about it. Leave him in no doubt about what *you* want. Then leave the rest to him.'

Cleo had never turned down a dare. She stood at the base of the trellis attached to the wall outside Jack's bedroom, chewing on her lower lip and toying with the zip on her black figure-hugging jumpsuit. Her new black lace bra and panties from Bedroom Secrets itched something fierce.

Lucky for her no one had ever asked for the impossible or even slightly dangerous.

Until now.

Now she was asking for it for herself. For Jack. For what they could have together if only he'd let it happen.

She knew she was risking a broken heart… A quick glance up had her amending that to maybe a broken neck? She figured it was worth it.

The moon was on her side for once, spilling light through the frangipani branches, clearly outlining her own personal stairway to heaven. She plucked a frangipani blossom and tucked it in her hair. Checked her watch by moonlight. Jack's room had been in darkness for fifteen minutes.

She wanted to give him time to be relaxed and receptive to her. Over the past few days she'd watched that self-contained, remote Jack take over. It was up to her to bring out the Jack she'd only glimpsed in the past two weeks.

The fun-and-games Jack who'd scaled this very trellis on that first morning, that sensitive guy who'd comforted and talked with her in Gerry's room after the fiasco with the will.

The drunk, dishevelled and definitely dangerous man who'd pushed her up against a wall and put his mouth on hers. The memory sent an instant shard of heat searing a path to her lower abdomen.

Since Jack obviously wasn't going to, she would take that next step towards intimacy herself. An intimacy that went so much deeper than the sexual act. A bond, she knew, that could never be broken, no matter where in the world he went, no matter how hard he tried to deny it.

Nerves pinched her skin and fluttered in her tummy as she contemplated the climb. 'Okay, Jack,' she murmured, placing a bare foot on the first rung and gripping it with her toes. 'Ready or not, here I come.'

CHAPTER EIGHT

CLEO SWUNG UP onto the first rung. Her pulse raced, a nervous excitement jittered up and down her spine. She climbed steadily upward, concentrating on not looking down. She'd seen Jack do it with an injured shoulder, how hard could it be?

But her palms were damp, her heart seemed to have lodged in her throat. Branches tapped lightly at the ground-floor window. Somewhere she could hear party music, the thump of bass on the air in time with blood pounding in her head. Just a few more feet…

Uh-oh. Wrong window. Of the two windows in his room, contrary Jack had left the wrong one open… *Don't look down.*

She looked down.

Her head spun nastily. No way could she go back the way she'd come. The white-knuckled fingers of one hand clung to the trellis while she pried one hand off to tap at the pane. 'Jack.' Her voice came out barely above a whisper. She was afraid if she raised it, somehow she'd be flung from the wall and land in a heap below. A *broken* heap. She gritted her teeth and tried again. 'Jack.' Louder. Her whole body was taut as wire, aching with the tension of holding on.

A face appeared. Thank God. She almost wept with relief. 'What the hell?' it shouted.

So much for a dramatic entrance. 'It's me, Jack. Open up.'

The window shot up with a sharp riff and Jack leaned out, peering at her over the window ledge. 'God, are you crazy?'

Not just a face. A body. A very *naked* body from what she could see. 'Just help me in, Jack.' Calm voice. Calm, in control voice. Not-so-calm pulse.

Two strong arms reached out, lifting her bodily through the opening as if she weighed no more than the shadows surrounding her.

'Thanks.' Her valiant attempt to appear nonchalant failed miserably as her legs turned to jelly. She clutched those, strong safe arms while her chest ached and her lungs burned from holding her breath.

'What in hell do you think you're doing?' he demanded in a dangerously low voice.

The bright slash of moonlight carved an equally dangerous expression on his face; his arms, shoulders, chest could have been painted with it. His eyes glittered, smoke and silver in the dimness.

'I wanted to see you…' *Wrong choice of words. Wrong, wrong, wrong.*

Her gaze kind of slid downwards. And stuck. An instinctive feminine awe speared through her body. Her blood turned to quicksilver in her veins. It looked…*he* was…magnificent. And growing more magnificent even as she watched.

'Congratulations,' he said tautly, his voice thick. 'I think we could say you've achieved that.'

He tilted her chin with a thumb and finger till she had no choice but to look into those dangerous eyes and not at the action taking place below.

'Listen, and listen good, Cleo. Don't you *ever* try anything like that again.' He tightened his grip on her chin. 'Understood?'

'No, not understood.' She batted his hand away. 'You give yourself permission to take risks and I'm not supposed to? And don't give me any of that chauvinistic crap because I'll refuse to discuss it.'

His lips firmed into a blade-thin line. 'Okay. Have it your way. For now.'

'I…' Her voice hitched, then trailed off as her breath rushed in and out. The traumatic ascent and the sight of all that masculinity had made her light-headed, and her whole body trembled.

'Come on, sit down before you fall down.' Sweeping her off her feet, he deposited her on the side of the bed, managing to drag the sheet around his hips at the same time.

His hand wasn't steady as he switched on the bedside lamp at its lowest setting, surrounding them in halo of soft amber light. He drew a deep heartfelt breath and let it out slowly, watching her in a way that had her stomach twisting into knots again.

'If you wanted to see me you could've tried the traditional method and used the door,' he said at last.

'It was a dare; I didn't have a choice.'

'Who the—'

'I challenged myself. I figured you'd take more notice this way.'

He shook his head and she saw the tension in his features relax a little as a corner of his mouth quirked. 'So is it Cat Woman, or Tropical Island Barbie?' he asked, touching the flower she'd forgotten.

'Barbie?'

'Your hair's just like that Barbie doll you had as a kid—of course that's only the visuals,' he hurried to explain. 'Comes from working behind the camera.' He leaned forward and sniffed, rubbing the tips between his fingers. 'But the feel and scent's your own.'

'Gee, thanks.'

He cocked his head. 'You're like a young Goldie Hawn; all sleepy eyes and hair.'

'I'm not sleepy now.'

She should have done something different with her hair. Barbie or Goldie was *not* the look she'd tried for, and both were decades older than her. She'd hoped to look like one of his models—sleek and sophisticated. Like Liana what's-her-name. Impossible given Cleo's generous breasts and lack of height.

But a week ago he *had* looked at her; he had kissed her.

He had wanted her.

And she'd wanted him. It had been sheer torture to step back before he did. A win for her.

Now all she had to do was keep that upper hand.

Keep it light. She touched the zip tab lying between her breasts. Imagined Jack's hand closing over hers…

He'd lower the zip an inch at a time and find the black lace bra. His long fingers would slide over the top of her breasts, then lazily back and forth before dipping beneath the lace. Taking it slow, driving her wild with wanting.

But she'd wait, because she wanted it to last. He'd find her nipple and she'd sigh as he rolled it gently between his fingers, pushing the lace aside to lower those hot, full lips and… Yes!

No. She bit back a moan of frustration. As if he'd read her thoughts, he leaned away, putting his weight on one hand on the bed behind him. Backing off.

'So…' he began. 'You wanted to see me about…?'

'Us, Jack.' Ignoring the inner voice whispering that he wasn't exactly falling into her plan, she forged on. 'I've been thinking, *for myself*, and I've decided what's right for me.'

She was going to seduce Jack. Oh, God, had she really been thinking that? Her stomach turned a double somersault. The Jack who'd be all too familiar with seduction, who'd had a string of beautiful women, who lived his life on his terms, as he chose.

The Jack who looked a little nonplussed right now as her presence in his room, her little speech—and the implication—penetrated.

His free hand crept up to rub at his neck. 'I think—'

'Don't.' She reached for the medallion, felt a rush of heat as her fingers brushed soft, masculine hair.

Metal winked in the light and was warm from his skin. 'Don't think, don't say anything. Listen. Why do you still wear this misshapen, unevenly forged scrap of metal?'

He opened his mouth to speak, but she tugged at the chain, bringing him closer. His breath whispered over her face. 'I said listen.'

Eyes darker than midnight locked on hers as she placed the medallion over his heart. 'Wherever you've been, I've been with you. Every woman you've slept with, I've been there, between you. Yet you still wear it, next to your heart. What does that tell you, Jack?' She could feel its fast thud beating beneath her hand.

'Cleo…'

'I'm not done yet. I want you to think back to that last night.' Those whirligigs in her stomach were spinning like windmills now, but it was a powerful feeling, having Jack at a disadvantage.

She leaned nearer. He leaned away. She could smell his soap, his skin, could see the muscles in his rock-hard abdomen straining as he struggled to remain upright. One gentle nudge and she'd have him right where she wanted him; on his back.

She laid her palm on that corrugated-iron belly and felt his muscles tighten as he sucked in air through his teeth. His eyes flashed a warning. She paid no heed as her hand crept higher, lightly over the ridge of newly healing scar tissue, then moving on to explore chest hair and one flat male nipple.

A sigh barely escaped his lips as she circled the soft areola with her fingernail. 'Are you still thinking about that night?' she reminded him. 'I was waiting for you. Did you ever wonder who stowed the rug and champagne in your car, Jack? Who organised the "Slow Dance Favourites" CD when it was my turn to dance with you?'

'I guess I know now,' he said, fingers closing around hers so she could no longer touch him. His thumb chafed her palm, the sensation exquisite torture. 'You decided Sam was a better option.' There was more than anger and accusation in his tone.

'I used Sam. Shamelessly. Stupidly. I realise that now. I wanted you to notice me.'

'Oh, I noticed all right.'

She threaded the fingers of one hand through his soft hair and pressed a kiss to the corner of his mouth. 'I was trying to make you jealous. Did you even figure that out?'

'I had no right to be jealous.' The hand holding hers tightened on the last word.

'*Were* you jealous, Jack?'

'You were sixteen, Cleo, for God's sake!'

'You haven't answered my question.'

He released her hand to swipe at his neck. 'You were sixteen; that *is* the answer.'

'Dear Jack.' She splayed a hand against his chest. 'Stubborn as ever.'

And with that promised nudge he slid bonelessly back onto the mattress. In one quick smooth motion, Cleo flicked the sheet aside. And went weak all over. Her hand fell away. Her mouth dried, her pulse picked up as excitement stabbed through her.

He was all fully aroused, heart-stopping male. From the powerful jut of his thick sex, the broad chest, to the tight, stubbled jaw.

He projected an image of laziness, but she felt the lethal undertones, like a lion ready to spring into action. And…in this position, he was also vulnerable.

With fingers that shook annoyingly, she kept her eyes on his while she lowered her zip to her navel. Her lace-covered breasts spilled out. For all the good it did; his eyes didn't leave hers—unreadable—but the muscles in his jaw were clenched, the tendons in his neck stood out and his breath was forced and harsh.

Slowly she lowered her upper torso to his, and, letting instinct guide her, moved against him. She rubbed her belly against his hip and watched the way his mouth moved. Silently, as if he was swearing. Or praying.

She caught his face between her hands, saw his eyes widen, darken. With a dizzying rush she felt an awesome female power she'd never experienced swell within her.

'I'm not sixteen now,' she breathed. And pressed her lips to his. They were warm and full and luscious and she was going to have him on toast for breakfast. The only barrier was her faux-leather suit, but as she moved against that hard wedge of masculine flesh she felt it buck. His hands fisted in the sheet.

He made no attempt to reciprocate, but neither did he push her away. Encouraged, she slid her tongue along the seam of his tight mouth and sampled his taste.

Jack didn't budge. Didn't dare. He'd left his retreat too late. Any movement would cause friction between their bodies and set off a chain reaction he didn't want to think about. His rock-hard erection strained and chafed as that slippery catsuit tormented and teased. Every muscle in his body, every square centimetre of skin, every cell, burned.

She changed the angle of the kiss and rubbed up against him like an eel, her warm, slippery length sliding over his thigh, the soft pillow of her breasts a sinuous, torturous caress against his chest.

His angel in temptation's clothing.

Her mouth was sweet sin, the kind that made a mere mortal man want to sin some more. A lot more. He clung to the hope that he had at least a shred of integrity left in his heat-ravaged body.

But the taste of her tongue as it explored the shape of his mouth was dark and rich and seductive. He felt the slow slide towards surrender as he drew it into his mouth to tangle with his in a slow, deep dance that had him straining for another kind of slow and deep.

Her hand left his face to trace a scorching path down the front of his body; over nipples, ribs, abdomen... His sex jerked at the first touch of her hand, then she slid her thumb over the moist tip and he teetered on the edge of madness.

With the strangled sound of a drowning man, he tore his lips from hers. 'Cleo,' he whispered.

Her hair fell in a silky curtain of moonshine as she lifted her head and leaned over him. 'Yes,' she whispered. 'It's me.'

With the practised art of a seductress, she brought those wet fingers to her mouth while she watched him. She licked them slowly with the tip of her tongue, one at a time, leaving them glistening. 'You taste good, Jack.'

His mouth fell open; rational thought deserted him. Then, God help him, she enclosed him again in that sleek wetness. 'Stop!' A second longer and he'd embarrass himself into her hand. He lurched up.

She stopped. 'Did I hurt you?'

'No. Yes, no. *Hell!*'

'I'm not doing it right. I don't...I'm not...' Her glazed, passion-filled eyes stared into his.

Innocent eyes. He grabbed her wrist, held it as far away as his trembling arm allowed. Had she lied that last night in his room?

They remained in that gridlock for several long, tension-filled seconds, their eyes fused. His body was ready to explode, his breath ragged and he knew his hand grasping hers was shaking.

'All that self-control's not healthy, Jack.'

'But necessary.' He cleared the sandpaper rasp from his throat. 'A dare's one thing; this...*this* is...'

'What I want; what you want,' she finished for him.

Fighting a battle he was rapidly losing, he shook his head. As soon as probate was granted and he was satisfied all was well, he was gone. He could give her that, if nothing else.

'Goldilocks...' He loosened his death grip on her wrist to soothe the satin-smooth flesh. Her face was flushed with anticipation, her lips rosy from the kiss.

The kiss that shouldn't have happened. Wouldn't have happened if he'd acted sooner. 'What I want has nothing to do with what's right and fair,' he said.

The passion in her eyes turned dark, her arm tensed beneath his hand. 'To hell with that.' She looked pointedly at his throbbing erection, which only made him ache more, then back to his face. 'You don't want me to go.'

'We are *not* doing this.' The denial came out harsh and forced. The air simmered between them, a brooding stew of hot emotions and unfinished business.

Then she dropped her gaze to her own lap, her shoulders drooped and he felt her pain right down to his toes. 'So…' she said. 'I came on to you—totally not your fault—but when it comes right down to it, I'm not good enough.'

She was so wrong. And that was the killer, testing his resolve down to the wire.

'Cleo, Goldilocks…that's not true, you were…' *Back off now.*

Her Cat Woman suit made a shooshing noise as she slid to the edge of the bed. Unshed tears shimmered in her eyes, tiny diamonds on her lashes, but blue fire burned in their depths. 'No need to explain. I know home-town girls aren't to your taste.'

His fingers itched to wipe the damp away. Face it, his fingers itched for entirely more basic reasons. His self-disgust was complete. Here he was imagining how it would feel to touch her, really touch her, when she was hurting and humiliated. She was better off not knowing how he felt, how he ached.

She patted his hand, making him feel like a total bastard. 'I'll leave. I've always been real good at making a fool of myself in front of you. I should be used to it by now.' She rose, hands fisted at her sides. 'Think of me when you're lying here alone tonight. For that matter, you can spend the rest of your life being right and fair. And *alone*.'

She shook her head when she reached the door. 'But I guess you won't be alone for long, will you, Jack?'

And while his brain tried to catch up with the rest of his body, she slipped away.

Jack dragged the last box from his father's wardrobe and sat on the floor to sort through it. It had been a huge job over the past two weeks, sorting clothes for the Goodwill box, hours on the phone and in Scott's office going over paperwork so all would be in order for Cleo.

He'd taken long jogs around the neighbourhood and spent hours at the local gym where he'd punished his body till there had been no room for thought.

His shoulder had healed well enough to join the basketball match last week, but Cleo had begged off, pleading a migraine.

When they had shared a meal—the only thing they seemed to share these days—they had talked like strangers. Polite, distant. The subject of their relationship remained off limits for both of them, something he'd have to deal with before he left. He couldn't, *wouldn't* leave without addressing Cleo's loss of self-esteem.

He missed her sunny, outgoing personality, her

forthright nature. Who else could put him in his place the way Cleo did? He missed her smile at the breakfast table. She was in her workshop before six o'clock most mornings and often managed to be elsewhere when he was around.

Could he blame her? Blowing a harsh breath, he lifted the lid. Sixties *Rolling Stone* magazines and paraphernalia. He put them aside for the recycling bin and looked deeper.

Photos. Black and whites. His father had preferred to work with the drama of shade and light, whereas Jack liked the vividness and immediacy of colour. Jack had learned photography by osmosis—one of the few positives he'd inherited from his father.

He sifted through some nudes, all of the same woman—a well-endowed brunette. Dad's? Then he frowned. The last one was of Jack in a tux taken at his eighteenth with the brunette snuggled up against him. Naked. What the...? Disbelief plunged through him. Dad's handiwork, he realised. His father had enjoyed experimenting in the dark room. He'd merged two shots. Why?

Then he recalled the conversation. What had Cleo said? *You'd know all about photographing naked women... I've seen the evidence.* He clenched his fist around the photo and threw the crumpled paper at the wall. Bastard. Another one of his father's attempts to make Jack look bad in Cleo's eyes.

Disgust filled him. Was there no end to this man's hidden talents? This man who was his father.

Not for the first time another equally abhorrent

thought slid through his mind. He carried his father's genes. Jack never used his camera to lie, but the violence…

Agitated, he got up and prowled to the window. Hadn't Jack pounded anyone who had tried to put the moves on a young Cleo? Like the bastard who'd told Scott what he wanted to do with her. The satisfaction of bone crunching bone. The hot smell of blood. Did that make him a violent man?

Too right. He clenched his fist against the window pane till his nails bit flesh. Didn't matter that the other guy had thrown the first punch. An unenlightened Cleo had been appalled at Jack's behaviour when word had got out, whereas Dad hadn't batted an eyelid. Like father, like son.

Yet another reason to stay the hell away from Cleo.

No one had been good enough for her because *he'd wanted her for himself.*

The reason he'd left.

The reason he'd leave again.

Because he wasn't good enough either: *family and commitment.*

He hadn't needed to try very hard to keep his distance today. She'd breezed out this morning and he hadn't seen her since. He checked his watch—four p.m.

And wondered where she was now.

'We need a girls' night,' Jeanne said as she and Cleo strolled the mall licking ice-cream cones. Jeanne closed up shop at one p.m. on a Saturday, and they usually spent the afternoon together.

Cleo had reported her failed mission with Jack, and Jeanne obviously felt she should try to lift Cleo's spirits. 'Good idea,' Cleo said, feeling duty-bound to agree, even though she'd prefer to hole up in bed with a book or a mind-numbing bottle of red.

'Girls' night, as in *in* or *out*?' Jeanne asked before wrapping her tongue around her chocolate pecan ice-cream.

'Out. Definitely out.' Cleo took a chunk out of her raspberry-flavoured one. 'It's been three weeks since... Since Jack and Scott did the town. It has to be our turn.'

'You want cool and classy or hot and sweaty? As in nightclub hot and sweaty,' Jeanne added with a grin.

Images of Jack in the garden minus the shirt, his skin slick and gold in the sun while they turned soil for the sundial, snuck up to mess with Cleo's hormones. And as for the Cat Woman scene— *Don't go there. Don't go remotely near there.* Hormones were off limits. Jack was off limits. She'd humiliated herself enough.

'Cool and classy,' she said. 'I don't think I can cope with hot and sweaty of any kind right now.'

She stopped in front of one of the mall's fashion boutiques, attracted by a low-cut watermelon-pink top and matching handkerchief skirt. That didn't mean she couldn't dress hot.

She caught her reflection in the boutique window and frowned. Boring, boring, boring. The top she wore must be four seasons old. And she lived in jeans or overalls. How long since she'd splashed out on something feminine? Something that would knock Jack's eyeballs to the back of his head.

She lifted a shoulder. Not that she cared what he thought. *Liar.* More like she wanted Jack to see what he was missing out on. 'I wonder if they have that outfit in my size,' she said, and, handing her ice-cream to Jeanne, she went inside to ask.

Back at Jeanne's apartment, Jeanne twitched at Cleo's gauzy layers of skirt, then stepped back with a smile. 'Stunning with a capital S. You sure you don't want to go somewhere more crowded to show it off? Seems a waste to spend the evening eating seafood at Ritzy's with plain old Jeanne when you could have a nightclub full of men at your feet.'

Cleo did a slow turn in front of Jeanne's mirror, checking out the back view. 'I don't want men at my feet.'

'Okay, it doesn't have to be your feet.'

'Ha ha.'

But Cleo did feel a little like Cinderella going to the ball. The top fit like a glove, showing a flattering cleavage, hinting at more. Sparkles spilled down the single spaghetti strap and swirled over the bodice. Matching strappy pink stilettos completed the look, and underneath she'd purchased a strapless bra, and, in a daring move, a hot-pink thong. The chiffon skirt, with its six points of sheer fabric reaching just below the knee, gave the outfit a whimsical feel.

A warm glow of pleasure spread through her body. Not bad. Not bad at all.

Until she looked at her face.

Some of that pleasure dulled. She wasn't Cinderella,

she was still Cleo Honeywell. Worse, she was still Goldilocks. 'I need a fairy godmother with her magic scissors.' She turned to Jeanne. 'Will you cut my hair?'

'Sure, a quick trim would—'

'I mean *really* cut it—short as in...s-h-o-r-t.' She held up her thumb and forefinger an inch apart. She didn't tell Jeanne about the picture of Liana what's-her-name draped over Jack's arm with short, spiked, *sophisticated* hair.

The Goldilocks/Barbie image had to go.

'God.' Jeanne straightened, her expression one of astonishment. 'I'd kill for your hair and you want to cut it off? Have you thought about this? What'll Jack say? He's crazy about your hair.'

Barbie doll hair. Cleo turned away quickly and caught her own mutinous reflection. 'I'm not doing it for Jack.'

'Right,' Jeanne said. 'Bugger Jack, the man's an idiot. A woman should do what pleases her. Still, it's rather drastic.'

'I'm feeling drastic.' A new and exciting anticipation slid through her. She stripped off her new clothes.

Jeanne tossed her an old shirt. 'Okay, let's do it.'

A couple of hours later Cleo stood in front of her own mirror studying the transformation with a mix of horror and exhilaration.

She'd covered her hair in a sun hat and sneaked in, but she needn't have bothered. Jack was napping in front of the TV tennis while Sweden and the U.S. battled it out for the Australian Open.

Oh. My. God. She raised a hand to her hair. What there was of it. Jeanne had put highlights and something called styling mud through it and it stood up in soft little tufts all over her head.

She looked at the whole picture. The lack of hair seemed to augment her eyes; they looked brighter and lighter, and her diamanté studs actually showed.

She laughed out loud. It was totally *out there* along with body piercings and tattoos. And which of those would come first? Probably neither, since both involved pain, but it was satisfying to know she could. If she chose.

Today she'd made a decision solely for herself. It felt good, and liberating. She was definitely going to do it more often. She held the pink outfit aloft on its hanger and laughed again. Starting tonight.

Two hours later, fresh from a long scented bath and a careful make-up session, she watched Jack from the edge of the family room. He'd stretched out on the floor in baggy shorts and a T-shirt with the sleeves ripped out. One hand curled around a can of beer. His head was propped on a cushion and he was watching the TV news between the V of his long, sexy feet. His hair was mussed.

As she watched his free hand pushed the T-shirt higher, over hair-sprinkled, taut gold skin and scratched lazily back and forth.

Heat flashed through her blood. The thought of those long fingers cruising slick and slow over her own belly seared through her brain. She took a deep breath to calm herself. Another before she said, 'Jack, I won't be home this evening. There are a couple of frozen dinners you can microwave if you want.'

'Hmm...okay.' He didn't tear his eyes from the sports news.

'Don't wait up.'

He glanced her way, then seemed to turn to stone. His beer-can hand paused halfway to his lips.

Give him time to look, but not to ask questions.

She felt the slow slide of his gaze from the burnished, highlighted tips of her hair to her freshly lacquered toenails. Back to her head. Shock furrowed his brow, darkened his eyes. And something more—her skin prickled—something...hot.

'Your hair...'

'Jeanne did a good job, didn't she?'

'Ah...'

Slack-jawed and speechless. A first for Jack Devlin.

Keeping to her plan, she glanced pointedly at her watch. 'Gosh, is that the time? I've got to go.'

'Wait up...'

But she was already halfway across the room, her stilettos clicking over the tiled foyer. Timing was critical.

'Where are you...? I'll drive you.'

She beamed at him—over her *exposed* shoulder—as she reached for the door knob. 'No, thanks, I'm fine. Bye.' And pulled the door shut behind her.

She didn't know if Jack would come after her, but she did know by the heat on the back of her neck that he was watching from the window. Good. Great. Satisfaction had never felt so good.

Her mood lighter than it had been in a long time, she walked to her car without looking back. 'Enjoy your evening, Jack. I intend enjoying mine.'

CHAPTER NINE

JACK checked his watch for the umpteenth time, then punched the wall. Two a.m. Where the hell was she? Who was she with? Of more concern, what was she doing?

Forcing the unsettling images away, he went back to standing at his window in the dark, willing her car to turn into the drive. A gentle night breeze flirted with the curtain, cooling his naked, sweaty chest. He saw Con crouched on the porch like a great fur log with whiskers. The stillness of the night was interrupted briefly by a dog barking, the call of a night bird.

But no Cleo.

Her mobile was switched off. Why was it off? Letting out an impatient snarl, he slid to the floor and leaned back against the wall.

The image of her as she left was seared into his brain as clear as any photograph. How many times had he studied it tonight?

She'd cut her hair. What was all that about? And that outfit— Whew. His hormones kicked in again at the memory. He'd never seen her in anything so feminine, so…startling. So un-Cleo.

But he'd detected a glint of mischief in those big blue eyes. As if she knew something he didn't. He cracked his knuckles. He hadn't liked not being in control of that situation one bit.

Two-ten a.m. Blowing a harsh breath, he watched the streetlight and shadows play on the wall. Apart from a couple of evenings out with Jeanne, since he'd been back, Cleo hadn't been on a date.

Was this a damn date? Did she date regularly? He hadn't been around Cleo, the adult.

The woman.

The woman he'd held in his arms not so many nights ago. The woman who'd slapped his face, then scaled a wall to be with him. How could he not be moved by that unique spontaneity?

And, yes, he was going to stand by and watch someone else have her. Because it was best for Cleo. *Take a bow, Jack Devlin.*

So why was he sitting on the floor—while his bum went numb—counting the minutes?

The sound of a car's tyres had him scrambling up, his heart pounding with relief. But his relief was short-lived. When he looked down, an old Toyota Corolla with a dent in the front passenger side pulled up as the security light winked on.

He craned his neck—the car was directly below and the angle was wrong—but he could just see the pale but indistinct shape of two faces in the dimness.

His fingers curled on the window sill as a minute

ticked by. Two. Three. What was she waiting for? It became obvious when the two faces merged into one for a second or two.

Two seconds too long. The hot quick flash took him by surprise. *Not* jealousy. But it snaked through his body like venom. And still he stood, unable to turn away, while the passenger door opened with a groan of tired metal and Cleo stepped out, laughing at something lover-boy said.

She looked young and vulnerable with that short hair, her slender body reflected in the porch light. For a nerve-racking moment he thought she was going to bring him in too, but she pushed the car door shut and waved, disappearing from view as she stepped onto the verandah.

He pried his fingers from the sill, unclenched his jaw and ordered himself to get a grip. Take a cold shower. Go to bed.

But he wanted to see her again. Simple as that.

And just as simply, he turned and walked to his door to wait for her to come up to her room.

When she didn't come, he paced the floor, then—to hell with it—he stalked downstairs. He found her in the kitchen, pouring milk into Con's bowl while Con wound his way around her perfectly shaped legs. He had an insane urge to slide right on over and do likewise. All that exposed creamy skin made him think of warm milk and honey and how smooth and sweet it would taste against his lips.

Which made him scowl as he propped himself on the door jamb and crossed his arms over his chest.

'What's the point of having a mobile if you switch it off?'

She whirled, spilling drips of milk on the floor and over her hand. 'Jack!' She did a quick scan of his body—naked but for midnight-blue boxers—then concentrated too hard on the milk carton as she replaced it in the fridge. 'You're still up.'

'Yes.' More than she knew. Shifting to hide the augmenting evidence, he crossed his right ankle over his left. He stared hard at her until she met his eyes. 'The phone?'

'Oh. I only switch it on in an emergency,' she said. Her tongue darted out to lick the milk off her hand. Still holding his gaze. As if she knew what was going on a few hands lower and wasn't game enough to look.

He cleared his throat. 'How do you know if there's an emergency if you don't keep it on?'

'I mean, if my car breaks down, or something.' She ripped off a piece of paper towel and crouched to mop up the spill. Con lapped up the stingy milk offering and walked off in disgust towards the stairs.

'So…did your car break down tonight?' he asked in a reasonable voice.

She rose slowly, walked to the bin and tossed the paper. Then she leaned one hip against the counter. 'No, but I don't like the way you said that. It had a definite edge.'

'An edge.' She was trying to put the blame on him? His temper spiked. He reined it in, barely. 'Wasn't your car I heard pull up.'

'I had a couple of drinks. I left my car at Jeanne's.'

'Jeanne's?'

Her own temper fired up in those blue eyes. 'Why are my words coming back at me, and what's with the eyebrow lift?'

He shrugged. Let her dig herself into a hole. 'Wasn't Jeanne who drove you home.'

'No. It wasn't.' She watched him for a long moment. He thought he saw regret or hurt flicker across her features before she blanked all expression. 'Jack, you made it quite clear you didn't want me in your bed—'

'Bed?' Cleo naked beneath him, her pale body writhing on his black silk sheets… Before the erotic image could take hold he cut her off with a quick slash of his hand. 'Did I say anything about bed? I only mentioned a lift home.' He pushed away from the door. It wasn't only temper now, it was anger and pain and a load of other stuff he couldn't seem to sort out.

She toed off one pink shoe, then the other, shrank a couple of inches. 'I didn't think—'

'Obviously not.'

Without her shoes, she looked like a little girl lost with her raggedy hair and skirt. He wanted to take her in his arms and make everything all right. He wanted to shake her till she told him the truth.

Mostly he wanted to knock lover-boy's balls into his throat.

'Is that why you're late?' *Because you've been in some man's bed?*

She walked to the sink, took a glass from the drainer, filled it with water and drank it with her back to him.

'Before you rudely interrupted, I was going to say I didn't think it would matter to you. What I did. After all, you don't want me.'

He watched her slender bare neck as she rinsed the glass. *Not want her?* He should be relieved, even pleased. He'd achieved what he'd set out to accomplish.

So why did he want to hurl the nearest available object?

She reached for the tea towel and made a major production out of wiping her glass. 'That makes it none of your business, Jack.'

'The hell it doesn't.' His anger had claws. Anger at himself and anger at her because she made him forget. 'You're family, remember? That makes it my business.'

'No. I'm Cleo Honeywell, all by myself.' She turned her back on him. 'I'm nobody's business.'

'Wrong.' He slapped a palm on the table. Her words struck like a knife all the way to his soul. And he was responsible. She'd built a wall around herself to shut out the hurt. To shut out Jack Devlin.

He turned his anger on himself, raised a conciliatory hand towards her, let it fall, useless, to his side. 'You'll always be my business, Goldilocks.'

'Fat lot of good that'll do me on another continent,' she shot back in a voice that belied her small stature. 'Assuming I wanted your assistance, which I don't.'

In a lightning-quick move he was behind her. He could feel her heat, could see each tiny gold hair on the back of her bare neck. The subtle bouquet of feminine scents—perfume, shampoo, makeup—filled his head, leaving no room for reason.

All he knew was need.

She turned. Sucked in a breath as their bodies bumped. Wide, shocked eyes flew to his. Her breasts grazed his chest, the little beads on her top abrading flesh that was suddenly way too sensitive. If glass beads could do that, what havoc would warm bare skin and tight nipples wreak?

His hands streaked over firm shoulders, smooth arms. Grasping her hands, he brought them to his lips, slid his tongue over her palms, then the delicate inside of her wrists where her pulse beat like a fury. Her taste was all he'd imagined and more, sweeter than honey, smoother than milk.

And his eyes didn't leave hers. *I want to do this to you until there's not a patch of skin I haven't tasted.* He watched those eyes sharpen, deepen, saw the moment she registered his unspoken message.

'We have now,' he murmured. Then speech was beyond him. Waiting was beyond him.

Releasing her hands, he held her face between his palms. Saw his own arousal mirrored there in the flushed cheeks, lips parted in anticipation. He lifted her onto the counter top so they were eye to eye.

Then he set his lips on hers. Now had no beginning, it had no end. Now was all he needed, this moment, this woman, the hot, slippery slide of her tongue against his. At her soft moan he plunged deeper. She grasped his medallion, fisted a hand around it and tugged him closer.

She was in his head, his heart, his soul. Even in the

harsh glare of the kitchen light, by the night-darkened window and fully dressed, she surrounded him.

A strangled groan rumbled in his throat at the first whisker-light touch of her fingers over his chest, then again, God help him, when they scraped and rubbed over his nipples.

Sanity flew out the window, long-denied passion rushed in to fill the void.

Closer. More. More skin to skin. His hands trembled as they left her face and slid the single tiny strap off her shoulder, down her arm.

His senses absorbed the blur of hot-pink lace, soft flesh, the rasp of his own breathing as he unsnapped her bra, tossed it aside and filled his hands with the womanly weight of her breasts.

With his hands on her bottom, he slid her to the edge of the counter. He put his hands on the silky firmness of her thighs, pushed them apart and stepped between them. His erection came up hard against hot, damp panties.

'Jack.'

His name on her lips, breathy and demanding, drove need towards desperation as her hands clawed at his nape and her head fell back.

Then his mouth was on her neck. On that smooth, vulnerable place where the blood pounded like a drum and her moans hummed like music against his lips.

He was blind, deaf and dumb to everything but her. The warning voice thrumming at the back of his mind grew muffled, distant, until he could no longer hear it. Could no longer drum up the energy or the inclination to heed it.

He heard Cleo's voice against his ear, felt the brush of her breath as she said, 'So live the now, Jack. For once in your life let yourself go.'

Cleo's mind spun. Was she dreaming? Was this the Jack who'd tossed her out of his room not so many nights ago? Breathless, she put her hands on his shoulders, nudging him back so she could see him. She watched his eyes glaze over.

Right where she wanted him, and she hadn't even tried. The only way she'd known she'd ever get Jack in bed was if he wasn't thinking of consequences and all those other issues he had with her. Like now.

The urgent need to have that naked body—all of it—against her, in her, was like a fever in her blood. And the hot, hungry, almost unbearable anticipation had her squirming to get closer, her sweaty thighs sticking to the counter top.

As they watched each other he slipped an impatient hand under the strap of her thong. She felt a finger sliding along the moist folds, then inside her. She gasped and saw his eyes flash with heat and wanting. Her inner muscles contracted, liquid desire pooled as he manipulated her flesh with fast, flicking passes, but she grabbed at his hand. 'Not here,' she managed.

'Where?'

Every pulse point hammered out a primitive beat at his feral growl. *Somewhere close.* 'Family room.' She wrapped her trembling legs around his waist, her arms around his neck, and he dragged her off the counter into his arms.

Half walking, half stumbling, Jack made it as far as

the doorway. Her breasts were flattened against his chest. She wiggled, wanting more friction between their bodies. More Jack.

He pinned her against the door jamb to devour her mouth once more, then released her slowly. She slid down between cool, smooth wood and the hard, hot length of him. He wrapped a hand around the back of her neck, his fingers pressed against her flesh. 'You make me weak.'

Upper body gleaming in the slant of light from the kitchen, he looked anything but weak as he hooked a finger in the thong. And tugged. She felt callused palm and silk slide down her inner thighs. The scrap of fabric pooled at her feet and she toed it aside.

He shoved his boxers down and oh…my…God. A fully-primed-and-ready-for-action weapon. And she had no doubt it had destroyed more than its fair share of the female population.

He'd slept with so many beautiful, experienced women. She wasn't beautiful or experienced, and she felt a quick lick of fear that he'd find her lacking.

But that didn't seem to be a problem for him right now. In the slant of light from the kitchen he looked like a bronze sculpture. A wickedly gorgeous, delicious male sculpture who was obviously more than capable of doing wickedly gorgeous, delicious things to her.

Her legs turned liquid. She was pinned there by his hands on her waist and one power-packed, hairy thigh between her legs.

Hard and hot as molten steel, his thigh pressed

upwards against already sensitised flesh, the hair-roughened skin rubbing, abrading as he rocked against her, his breath coming in short, sharp bursts. Her back and head slapped against the wood. All she could do was hang on.

Fast hands rushed up her body, over her breasts, stroking, squeezing, kneading. Her fingers dug into his upper arms, and beneath her palms she could feel the bunched ropes of sinew and muscle.

He swore—a rough-edged, almost violent sound—and for one panic-filled moment she thought he was going to back out again and she'd have to kill him. But he crushed his mouth to hers again, and, with their lips locked, he lifted her, whirling her across the room as if they were performing some mad, erotic waltz.

They hit carpet, collapsed onto the floor in a tangle of limbs and pink chiffon. It broke the connection, but only for a second. There was a cool draught down on the carpet and the scent of summer roses from the vase on the coffee-table. She'd never smell roses again and not think of this moment and Jack.

The kitchen light was behind him, leaving his face in shadow. Only his eyes glittered in the dimness as they fused with hers. The glint of his watch caught the light as his hands shoved her skirt up to her waist, then raced over breasts, belly, thighs.

Lower.

Quick, clever fingers plunged hard and deep into her heat. Her breath caught at the shockingly intimate intrusion and she made a sound somewhere between a whimper and a purr. But she wanted this, wanted more. Wanted all.

Her thighs fell open under his skilled assault. He knew his way around a woman's body. Knew where to stroke, how to rub, and—oh, God—he slid his knuckles back and forth along her quivering flesh until her bottom lifted off the floor. 'Jack!'

She was flying apart, hurtling towards the edge of the world and didn't know if she'd ever find her way back. Reaching down, she rode his hand to anchor herself.

Then his mouth was on hers again, hard and unforgiving. There was an edge of desperation in the way his tongue invaded her, as if he were battling a war he'd wanted no part in. Arching her back, she willed him to love her as she was and let it be enough.

Abruptly he reared up, shoulders broad and dark as he rolled on top of her, his heavy thighs pushing her legs even wider. She felt the smooth, wet and hot tip of his erection against her exquisitely aroused inner flesh.

He looked into her eyes for a freeze-frame of time. And they were children again, poised on the edge of innocence.

In one long, liquid thrust he drove into her. The breath left her lungs in a whoosh; her inner muscles contracted around him as she struggled with the shock and speed of that first penetration.

He went absolutely still. She could feel his heat throbbing inside her. His hands gripped her hips, holding her prisoner while his eyes turned molten. 'Why didn't you tell me?'

'It's okay; I'm okay. *Please.*' She arched against him once more, drawing him further inside her. Already she wanted that urgent thrust of carnal power and heat again. And again and again.

Slowly he withdrew, creating a delicious friction and anticipation, then plunged deep a second time. *Yes.* A third.

She moved with him, learning his rhythm as if her body had been tuned to his, only his. His head dropped to her breast, his mouth suckling and feasting as their hips slapped together in perfect unison.

She ploughed her hands through his short silky hair, clenched them as pleasure built and swirled like ribbons through her body.

She wanted to stay here for ever, with Jack a prisoner inside her body, the cool blanket of night to protect them and the rest of the world asleep.

She was hot, so hot, her skin slick with perspiration, yet she shivered with every thrust, every glide of his tongue, every stroke of his hand. Each new sensation brought new delight and took her higher.

Harder, quicker, deeper, in perfect synchronicity, dancing to music only they could hear. The tempo grew wild, a primal beat that echoed in her blood, in her mind, until there was nothing but Jack, sweat-slick skin and hot, shallow breaths.

He tensed suddenly, his muscles quivering as he supported his weight on his arms, watching her, the tendons in his neck and shoulders standing out like ropes.

The ribbons of pleasure swirled low in her belly,

then coiled. She was back on the edge of the world, but this time she wasn't alone. And when she took that final leap, he poured himself into her still-pulsing body and was with her all the way.

Jack watched Cleo sleeping in the pre-dawn dimness, pale and luminous as a pearl on black velvet, her head against his shoulder, one hand curled on his chest. Some time ago he'd carried her to his room, a rag doll in his arms.

His jaw tightened and an ache spread through his body. Her crumpled dress on the floor was a stark and appalling reminder of what they'd done. What *he'd* done.

Cool, dew-scented air wafted through the windows and the silence in the house was absolute. As real and absolute as his self-contempt. Not only had he let his body do the talking instead of his brain, he hadn't used protection.

He hadn't used protection.

Of course, he hadn't come downstairs with the intention of having sex, but when he'd seen her bending over the cat the rational part of his brain had simply shut down.

Her legs beneath the hot-pink hide-and-hint skirt had made him want to pant. But he'd held it together. Hadn't he restrained himself from salivating at the sight of her newly bared neck, a particular weakness of his?

Until she'd laid that all-by-myself none-of-your-business crap on him.

All his self-talk, all his noble intentions had flown out the window. He'd lost it, plain and simple.

She'd been his business since the first day he'd laid eyes on the scrawny seven year-old with pigtails in her hair, a man-sized toolbox of scrap metal under her arm and the biggest blue eyes he'd ever seen.

For the past six years not a day had gone by when he hadn't thought about her. Until he'd left home he'd made it his duty to look out for her.

That made her his business.

No reason it should change now. Except that last night Scotty had told him that probate was final. The only thing missing was Cleo's signature on the documents and the estate was hers. She was an independently wealthy woman.

That didn't mean he *had* to exile himself. It only meant... He blew out a slow breath. What *did* it mean?

One thing for sure; everything *had* changed.

CHAPTER TEN

CLEO smiled as she surfaced into semi-wakefulness. Her body felt like molten gold. As if Jack were the metal-smith and had forged the ordinary into something shiny and beautiful.

When he shifted, she protested with an indistinct, 'No.' She wanted his weight on her, his body joined to hers a little longer. A lot longer. Her limp hands slid bonelessly up and over the hard curve of his shoulders.

'So this is what all the fuss is about,' she murmured, nuzzling her face against his chest, hearing the ponderous beat of his heart.

Making love.

Making real love.

If only tonight, the Now, could last for ever. She breathed in the musky warm air between their bodies that smelled of their lovemaking, and opened her eyes. The half-dream fled. Bright early morning light tinged with pink already flooded the room.

Jack's room.

Jack's bed.

Jack's body beside hers, *not* joined.

'You let me fall asleep,' she accused him, still hung over with sleep. Oxygen starvation probably had something to do with it since her nose was buried in his chest hair. 'Did I miss anything?'

She wriggled upwards till they were nose to nose, bellies brushing, and not only bellies… Feeling adventurous for so early in the morning, she traced a finger down the line of their bodies, and moulded her hand around him.

It bucked against her as if it were a living thing with a mind of its own—probably why they said men thought with their—

A sound rumbled in his chest and he closed a hand over hers. 'Cleo…' He drew both to his lips, entwining their fingers. 'We have to talk.' He said it as if they were discussing the economy rather than sharing body heat.

Ignoring the tone, she kissed the sexy stubble on his chin. 'No talk.'

'Yes talk.'

A huge ball of uncertainty lodged in her chest. 'Don't you *dare* apologise.'

'I could have made you pregnant.'

'Oh.' Relief washed through her, easing tensed muscles. 'Is that all?'

'Is that all? You don't think that might deserve an apology?'

'There's no chance of pregnancy; I'm on the pill.'

His expression didn't soften or relax. It remained grim, perhaps even grimmer.

Her muscles tensed again. 'Ah…after the Sam thing and my ladder trick, I suppose you'd be forgiven for jumping to conclusions, but it's a female problem. The doctor said the pill should correct it. And it did; I—'

'Are you…were you…' he seemed to struggle with the words '…last night, was I the first?'

Last night had been…hot and fast and furious, against the wall, on the floor…

Heaven.

But she supposed he could feel bad if he thought she'd been a virgin, which she *almost* had been—if such a thing were possible. She pressed her lips together, then asked, 'Does in and out count?'

She almost smiled at his hard-edged confusion when he frowned and said, 'Want to explain that?'

'Just what I said. One in, one out.' She shuddered at the memory of that bungled encounter. 'Once was enough.'

His eyes darkened. 'Sam?' She shook her head. He didn't look appeased. 'Did he hurt you?'

'No.' Not so much body as heart. 'I thought I wanted it, thought if I closed my eyes and imagined…'

'Imagined what?'

That it was you, you idiot. But she only shrugged her shoulder and said, 'Can't remember now.'

After that terrible, mortifying night she'd known it could only be with someone she loved. And she loved Jack Devlin. Only Jack. With an ache so big, so wide, so high, she wondered that her heart didn't burst out of her chest.

So tell him, whispered a little voice.

But how would he react to that profound piece of news? How would he rate his feelings for her on the love scale? She really didn't want to know. Because, no matter what he said, she knew he didn't want anything permanent, and long-distance love wasn't her idea of happy-ever-after.

'Who was your first, Jack?' She stroked his collarbone, turning attention on him and away from her inner pain.

His lips twitched as he remembered. 'Kitty Cartwright.'

'Oh, my God.' Cleo couldn't hide the grin. 'The photographer's apprentice. So, who apprenticed who?'

'I'll leave that for you to consider. Are you going to fill me in on yours?'

'Not on your life. My first time was last night.' She met his eyes. Last night's heat and speed still vibrated along her nerve endings and shimmered in the air between them.

Jack cupped her face in one hand. 'I shouldn't have been so rough on you.'

'I wanted rough; I asked for rough.' She closed a hand over his. 'In fact, I think I begged.'

'Ah, Cleo,' he murmured. 'I thought that was me.' As if in apology he lowered his lips for one long, soul-destroying kiss that stole the breath from her lungs.

His hard, masculine body slid over hers while his soft, full lips nipped at her chin, her neck, then closed hungrily over her mouth.

She melted under his hands as they warmed and teased. Not rough this time, but slow and deliberate, seeking out all the places that begged to be touched: her breasts, nipples, the hollow at the top of her thighs, just a scant fingertip away from her—

'Jack?' Scott's voice. Scott's face peering at them from the open doorway. 'You through with those…' The sound of a throat clearing. 'Morning.'

Cleo stiffened, appalled. She'd invited Scott to breakfast and here she was laid out like the main course. The warm, melty feeling disappeared. Now it was a warm, flushed, embarrassed feeling from head to toe and every place in between.

When she tried to push up to cover herself, Jack's body prevented her. Without looking at the morning intruder, he stopped his busy hands, and he raised his head enough to swear against Cleo's mouth. 'Ever hear of knocking, Scotty?'

'Sorry. I'll make coffee. Hi, Cleo.'

'Make it a long black,' Jack called back as Scott retreated down the corridor. 'Very long. How did he get in?' Obviously not embarrassed about being caught in the act, he took up nibbling where he'd left off. 'And what's he doing here on a Sunday morning at nine a.m.?'

'He and Jeanne both…have keys, and I invited him—*them*, actually. But Jeanne couldn't make it.' Jack was kissing his way over a breast, making it hard to concentrate. 'The three of us often have…' her breath hitched '…Sunday brunch.'

'I'd've thought brunch leaned more towards eleven a.m. onwards.'

'Ummm.' Frustrated with the interruption, she puffed out a sigh. 'Jack…'

'You don't want to continue this right now, do you.' A statement, not a question. He rubbed her arm before rolling off her.

'I can't—not with Scott prowling around downstairs.' Probably tripping over her discarded underwear. Her very new, very sexy underwear.

Her morning-after glow had been tarnished. Suddenly she felt more than naked. She felt exposed, and wished they were in the familiarity of her own bedroom.

'I'm going to take a shower,' she said, getting up and grabbing his sheet from the bottom of the bed. No way was she making that trek down the passage bare-bottomed.

'You know, we could share a shower,' he said with a sexy lift of his brows.

She paused as she adjusted the sheet over her shoulder. The idea had appeal. They could lock the door and…

His eyes took a leisurely stroll over her sheet-clad body. 'I could wash your back for you.'

'Mmm.' Not nearly as exciting as having her front washed, but she'd take what she could get.

She made her own journey over Jack's still relatively unfamiliar terrain. Taut, tanned skin stretched over muscle and bone, the little dip in his navel and the not-so-little jut of masculinity that beckoned every female cell in her newly awakened body.

Her eyes flicked to his face and the more familiar but no less arousing sight of that brown-eyed gaze, looking at her in an entirely new way, deep and penetrating.

Like last night.

And if she stood here any longer she was going to do much more than look. With an effort, she moved to the door, tossed a sexy glance over her shoulder. 'I'll bring my own soap.'

A few minutes later, clutching her toiletries and some hastily hunted-up clothes, she made her way back to Jack's room. The sound of his voice had her hesitating at his door. He was on his mobile phone and using that voice he reserved for women.

'Just some of those complicated family issues to resolve,' she heard him say. He nodded at something the caller said, throwing in a sexy laugh for good measure. 'Yes, I'm still interested. Very interested…' Pause. 'Tomorrow?' Another pause. 'Eleven-fifteen, Café Medici. I'll look forward to it. Ah. Can we keep this just between us for now?'

Cleo swallowed over the sudden grip on her heart. *Just between us.* But she stepped away, turned, and, hugging her bundle, fast-tracked back to her room. Closed the door. The fragrance of the Yves Saint Laurent soap she hoarded for special occasions filled her nostrils. It was a painful but necessary reminder that this might not be a special occasion for playboy Jack.

Did tigers change their stripes? She walked into her bathroom and turned the shower on full blast. She was probably being paranoid, but she'd wait to see if he was going to let her in on his secret rendezvous. *Okay, Jack. Let's see how you play this. Then I'll know.*

* * *

'Is that what I think it is?' Scott said as Cleo entered the kitchen.

She snatched up her thong at the doorway and her bra from the counter, averting her eyes from the man who knew too much, and sighed. 'You tell me.'

'It looks like Black Forest cake.'

She looked up. He was standing in front of the open refrigerator.

He licked a finger. 'Tastes like Black Forest cake.'

'Go ahead, it's all yours,' she said, looking for a spot to hide her undies. She gave it up—what was the point?—and put them on a chair.

He cut off a wedge. 'Want some?'

'I'll stick to fruit and coffee.'

'That doesn't sound like the Cleo I know.'

'Maybe I'm not the Cleo you know.' She took a knife and plate to the breakfast bar, sat down on a stool and reached for an orange.

'I've been trying to figure out who you look like without the hair. Tinkerbell,' he decided.

'Great.' So much for sophisticated.

'What does Jack think?'

'I'm not sure.' She wasn't sure about anything where Jack was concerned any more.

'So…' Scott set his cake down and sat on the stool beside her. 'You and Jack, huh?'

The fresh tang of citrus scented the air as she sliced her orange. They couldn't pretend nothing had happened, but she so didn't want to discuss it with Scott right now. 'Can we talk about something—'

'Where did you get to, Goldilocks?' Jack breezed in as if nothing had changed. He nuzzled her neck briefly, his soapy smell reminding her of the shower she *hadn't* shared, and whispered, 'Get rid of Scott. I want to talk to you—among other things,' then nicked a slice of her orange.

She watched him suck at it while he poured coffee. The long, hard length of him was now casually covered in shorts and T-shirt, but she could still see him last night, against that door less than a meter away. Naked, primal and fully aroused. The tiger and his stripes.

He'd been sucking her with the same enthusiasm. A tide of hot flushes washed through her as her body remembered and responded.

She was still watching and remembering when he stopped in mid-pour and frowned, his attention drawn to something beyond the window.

'Scotty?' He jutted his chin in the direction of his glare. 'Whose car's that?'

'The Corolla? It's a friend's. I lent him my car for the weekend. Had to drive his mother to her sister's in Ballarat.'

'So you drove Cleo home last night. Thanks.'

'No worries.'

Jack continued to top up his coffee, but Cleo saw the tension in his shoulders ease. In fact he looked extraordinarily pleased, she thought with a snarl as she picked at her orange. Smug, even.

Did the man always get what he wanted? 'I'll be out back,' Cleo said, grabbing her coffee as she rose.

Jack looked up sharply. 'Hey, I thought…'

She met his eyes and acknowledged the heated look that told her exactly what he thought. 'I'm behind in my commissions. I need to clock up some work hours.' *And you have something to tell me.* Or did he?

His lips curved in a sexy grin. 'Perhaps I can help.'

She nodded. 'Perhaps you can.'

'Wait up,' Scott said, reaching for the file beside him on the table. 'Before you both disappear I need you to sign these papers. Then the estate's done and I can leave you alone for the rest of the day.'

Knowing how hurt and humiliated Jack must feel, Cleo gritted her teeth and replaced her mug carefully on the table. This morning had taken another turn for the worse.

Jack sat in his father's big leather chair and scowled at the papers in his hand. He'd always avoided this room. This had been his father's domain, where he'd doled out verbal and physical abuse behind closed doors.

So why was he sitting in this monstrosity of an office when the woman in his life was a thirty-second walk away?

Because she'd told him she needed to work on her jewellery. He could understand her wanting some space. A simple signature and she had just become an unwillingly wealthy woman. He understood that.

But was that all that was bothering her? They'd both known the score on that point and he'd accepted it. Still, she'd seemed on edge when he'd joined her in the kitchen.

Was it the fact that they'd made love? He shook his

head. It wasn't her first time. He had to smile at her confession, and at the same time he had to hate the guy who'd taken what Jack had tried so hard to keep intact.

No. He'd noticed…something in those big blue eyes as she'd left for her workshop. Was it the Corolla moment? She'd managed to keep him guessing there. Perhaps she was disappointed he'd discovered her little secret.

The other reason he was here instead of trying to entice Cleo back inside and into his bed was because he'd also promised Scott some info a week ago and he'd promised to have it by the end of today.

Unfortunately it involved sorting through his father's filing system and desk drawers. He made a half-hearted attempt to start, then gave up, rolled the chair back and deliberately jammed his feet on the polished mahogany desk with its dark leather inlay.

His head was too crowded with thoughts and images of Cleo. The way those creative jeweller's hands had worked their magic on him, and her body so snug and so right against his. The scent and taste of her soft, milky skin, her sexy moans when she came—that had to be the most incredible moment of his life.

And the whole thing might not have happened if he hadn't seen her rock up in another man's car and panicked—Scott, as it turned out; the only man he trusted, the man he owed big time.

But Cleo was a family-and-commitment girl with her roots firmly in her home town whereas he needed to return to Rome, at least for a few weeks. He had obligations—Domenic and Carmela for starters. Carmela had informed him the old man was out of danger. He wanted to see for himself without a bullet in his chest.

But where was home? Not Rome. But for him, thanks to his father, home was a dirty word. Family was a dirty word. Jack loved the travel, the freedom of being his own boss, the love-'em-and-leave-'em credo he'd lived by for the first couple of years overseas.

Filming in war-ravaged areas had changed the way he looked at the world, and he'd been bound by a sense of duty he hadn't thought he'd had to stay and help. He'd thrived on the challenge.

Could he give all that up? And if he did, if he stayed...was he being fair to Cleo? With his father's violence and his mother's wanderlust in his veins, he was a bad bet.

Last night the cold, hard reality of seeing Cleo with another man in the shadowy confines of a car had tipped him over the edge. He lowered his feet and pushed away from the desk to pace. He'd lost it, big time. Lost control. Like his father. He struck a fist on the filing cabinet, tugged at a drawer. It opened with a sharp metallic sound. He had to get this done and get the hell out of his old man's office.

He dealt with the paperwork, saving a padded envelope Scott had handed him as he'd left today till last. As he sliced it open a gold key fell out, tagged 'lower desk drawer'. Fingers of tension gripped his neck as he studied the key in his hand. 'Okay, old man, what little surprise have you left me now?' Nothing pleasant, he was sure.

He fitted the key, opened the drawer and found a

letter addressed to him in his father's handwriting. Expelling a four-letter word, he considered tossing it out, but perhaps it had some info that pertained to Cleo or the estate.

The letter was dated six weeks before his death.

> Jack,
>
> As you read this, Cleo has inherited my estate. I knew I could count on your feelings for her to see it through.
>
> I understand why you didn't return sooner, even if Cleo doesn't. I made mistakes but I had my reasons.

'Is there a valid reason to beat your son?' Jack grated through his teeth.

> I fell for your mother knowing she was on the rebound. We married within a month and seven months later you were born. But I soon discovered domestic life didn't suit Atta. She was always off on some research caper or studying.
>
> Then after thirteen years of marriage she announced that our tenant, John Honeywell, and she were involved in more than research. Their decision to join that expedition to Antarctica meant dumping you kids. They just forgot to collect you on their return.
>
> Another surprise. Years ago a routine examination revealed I was firing blanks. I am not your father, Jack. Perhaps that helps you understand

why I could never love you; even before I found out, in my heart I knew.

As for Cleo—who wouldn't love her? And she was the only person who loved me for myself. You threatened that relationship. I did what I had to do to keep it.

Discovering you're only half a man makes one look at things differently. I needed a woman in my life. I needed Cleo.

You're wondering why I didn't pack you off to your mother when I discovered you weren't my son. You were already eighteen. Cleo adored you—she would have followed. I couldn't let that happen. But if I could convince her that you weren't worthy of her love…

Jack shook his head. 'You were one sick son of a bitch, Gerry Devlin.'

Finally, you won't be aware Atta and John first knew each other as uni students twenty-eight years ago. I met Atta after John took off on some overseas research scholarship. Make what you will of that.

Jack's fingers tightened on the paper. He'd been born twenty-seven years ago.

What you tell Cleo and how you deal with it is up to you. Perhaps you'll curse me for telling you, perhaps you'll thank me…

Jack didn't read any further. He couldn't seem to hold the paper steady. His stomach pitched and rolled; his eyes wouldn't seem to focus. Dates and years and calculations rampaged through his mind.

Think! But he didn't want to think. To think was to know. He slammed a fist on the desk. The glass lamp trembled. Papers sailed onto the floor as he swept them aside with a slash of his hand.

To *know*, was to know what his father was capable of. The part about John Honeywell had to be a lie. Deep down in some dark corner of his heart he knew it was a lie, but true to form, his father—*not* his father—Gerry had set him up to doubt. He refused to doubt.

But he had to be sure.

To do that he had to find his mother. Even if Honeywell hadn't been his mother's lover twenty-eight years ago, he couldn't put Cleo through the pain of knowing he was meeting her. Nor could he could tell her why.

Dad's—*Gerry's—coup de grâce*. *Your father could be my father.* The words shredded the very fabric of his life as he knew it, and he didn't know how he'd ever stitch it back together. 'Cleo.' Her name vibrated on his lips. She was the only thread that could save him.

He fumbled with the phone and had to punch in Scott's number twice. 'It's Jack.' He steam-rolled over Scott's cheery good morning. 'Drop whatever you're doing, I need your help.'

Fifteen minutes later, Jack had a bag packed, a seat

on the next flight to North Queensland, and Scotty's word to keep his mouth well and truly sealed. Thank God Scott the lawyer had his mother's address on file.

Depending on what he found he had to prepare for the possibility of severing all ties. Cleo could start a new life, be happy. Without him. That prospect wrenched at his heart till there was no room for anything inside him but pain.

He rang for a taxi, parked his bag by the front door and took a deep breath. All he had left to do now was inform Cleo he was leaving.

Therapeutic. That was what Cleo told herself as she pounded the sheet of metal. The forging hammer felt good and solid and familiar in her hand as she worked. Something she could control. An outlet for her emotions. She imagined it ran a close second to a punching bag.

She should be working on the silver and amethyst drop necklace she'd been fretting over for weeks, but it demanded intricate and exacting work, and she needed something more physical.

Which of course segued straight to Jack. She'd inherited what was his. That earned a chime of metal on metal that jangled through her hand and up her arm. She intended changing that as soon as Scott could do the paperwork.

Half an hour had passed and Jack hadn't come to talk to her about his coffee 'date'. Another clang. How could he make love to her as if she were the only woman in the world and arrange to meet another without telling her about it? Was she being paranoid? Probably.

'Knock knock.'

Cleo looked up, almost dropping her hammer with relief at the sound of Jack's seriously deep voice, and smiled. 'Hi.'

'I hope I'm not interrupting anything too complicated.'

Now he just sounded serious. A shadow seeped into her bones and her smile dropped away. She picked up a probe, began scoring the metal's surface and said, 'Would it make a difference?'

'This time? No. Cleo… I came to tell you I'm—'

'Leaving.' She closed her eyes.

One word to sum up Jack Devlin.

The loneliest word in the world.

He was going to put her out of his life now and move on. Like last time. No, not like last time, because this time he was taking more than her broken heart. He was taking the memories of one glorious night together—because she would *never* think of it again.

He was taking away hope. Her hope for a future with Jack, the home they could have shared, the babies they could have made…

Carefully, so he wouldn't see her hand shake, she swapped the probe for her hammer, ran it through her fingers, tapped it against her palm.

In the silence she heard the tinkle of her metal wind chimes outside the door, the neighbourhood sounds of someone's power tool and traffic and birds. Homey sounds. Sounds Jack didn't take the time to hear.

She forced herself to take one last look at him before she put him out of her mind, and her heart, for ever.

Dark—and was that troubled?—eyes met hers. The amorous, casual guy from breakfast had disappeared behind a stone façade.

His eyes flicked to the hammer she'd forgotten about. She tapped it against her palm again, harder, so that she felt the jolt sing up her arm. 'Someone beautiful offer you something better than love, Jack?'

He flinched at the word. She saw the stone wall crack a little and something infinitely sad clouded his eyes before anger took hold. 'Don't piss me off with crap like that. I'm coming back, Cleo, and we'll talk.'

'You know something, Jack? I don't want to talk to you, ever again. And I *want* to piss you off. I want to piss you off so bad that you never come back. And if you do, by some miracle, come back you won't find me here. Because I won't wait for you again.

'I love you, Jack Devlin. I love you more than I can say, more than you'll ever know. If I got down on my knees and humiliated myself some more and begged you to stay, or to take me with you, would you, Jack?'

His jaw tightened and he closed his eyes briefly. Then he lifted a hand, let it fall. 'Cleo, I—'

'Didn't think so. I'm through waiting for you. Goodbye, Jack.' Biting down hard on her lip to stop it trembling, she turned away and pounded metal to metal.

She didn't hear him leave, but a few minutes later, when her arm burned with the effort and she'd all but flattened her strip to smithereens, she realised she was alone again.

The knowledge left her reeling with grief. She wanted to love him, wanted him to love her, so desperately, so completely, she'd just shouted the word for all the world to hear—three times, for God's sake. *Idiot.* She threw her hammer across the room, then swiped a piece of pipe from her workbench and threw that too.

But Jack had never mentioned love. Jack was incapable of loving—he hadn't even mourned his father. One thing was certain; she couldn't stay here. *Wouldn't* stay here. Wouldn't be waiting for Jack if and when he decided to come back.

CHAPTER ELEVEN

'THANKS for letting me and Con stay here, Scott. You're a real hero.' Cleo was on hands and knees trying unsuccessfully to tempt the hulk from behind Scott's sofa with a bowl of chopped ham.

'No problem.'

She glanced up at the sombre tone to see Scott in the doorway, arms crossed and a frown line between his brows. 'Do you think Jase'll mind?' She had a sneaky feeling Scott's flatmate wasn't particularly fond of cats. Or of Cleo herself, for that matter.

'This apartment's half mine; it's okay.'

Not the answer she was hoping for, but Jeanne's tiny one-bedroom apartment didn't allow pets. And she absolutely, positively couldn't sleep alone in her house tonight. *Her* house. The reality only compounded her misery.

Giving up, she pushed the bowl towards the two eyes glinting in the dimness amongst the dust bunnies. 'I hope he finds the litter tray, he's not used to being inside all the time.'

'He'll find it,' Scott said, stepping away from the door. 'Come and sit down. We have to talk.'

Shifting an assortment of clothes to one end of the sofa, she let out a half sigh, half laugh. 'You mean I'll talk and you'll lend a sympathetic shoulder.'

'No, I have some things to say too and you need to hear them.'

Her attention snapped to the grim-faced stranger standing in the middle of the room. Scott had never sounded so terse. Not the same guy who'd turned up with banana caramel pie a couple of hours after Jack had left and saved her from herself. Suspicion narrowed her gaze. 'Jack put you up to this afternoon's tea party, didn't he?'

'He was worried about you.'

She snorted. 'Not worried enough to stick around or let me in on his plans.' Straightening, she said, 'I'm imposing; I'm sorry. I'll ring a cattery and book into a motel—'

'Your choice, but you'll hear me out first.' He jabbed a finger in her direction, his pewter eyes brooking no argument. So not Scott's manner.

Her surprise morphed into anxiety and some of those knots in her stomach tightened. She sat down. Scott remained standing. Okay, no sympathetic shoulder to lean on. 'All right, what's this about?'

'It's about Jack.'

She threw up a warning hand. 'If he wanted me to know, he would've told me.'

Scott shook his head. 'No. He wouldn't.'

His voice changed, making her super aware of the

vice squeezing her heart. Whatever Scott had to say, she didn't want to know. 'The trouble with Jack is—'

'Shut your mouth, Cleo.'

Reacting out of pure shock, she did.

'For once in your life listen to Jack's side.' He paced away towards the window where twilight was settling over the suburbs. 'It started about thirteen years ago...'

Cleo wrapped her hands around her knees, hugging herself in a dismal effort to contain the heartache. She felt the sofa dip as Scott sat beside her. He'd said plenty and now he didn't seem to have any words left. Nor could she get her own words out over the lump in her throat.

The man she'd loved as a father wasn't the man she thought he was. She felt numb, as if she were having the nightmare where she was running from something, only she couldn't move and it was dragging her down. She'd hit rock-bottom this time and there was no waking up. Today she'd lost not just one man she loved, but two.

She clenched her fingers till her nails bit into her palms. She wanted to lash out at someone. Anyone. Mostly she wanted to lash out at blind Cleo Honeywell. 'I should have seen it.'

'Don't blame yourself, Cleo.' She felt Scott's arm squeeze her shoulders in an attempt to comfort. It didn't. Nothing would.

'I should have known something wasn't right.' That Jack's bruises weren't always from backyard brawls, but something so much more sinister.

His father.

The man had abused his own flesh and blood.

'No one knew—Jack made sure of that. So did Gerry,' Scott finished.

All those years Jack hadn't let on. Cleo felt the burning sting of tears for what Jack had put up with. He'd stayed to look out for her. For the rebellious girl who'd given him grief at every turn. And when he had left—and she understood why now—he'd used Scott as back-up for her. Because he cared about her.

She'd been so wrong about him.

And like his father, she'd told him not to come back.

Cleo pushed off the sofa, rubbing her upper arms. She felt chilled to the bone despite the warm evening. 'You know where he is. Tell me, I must make it right between us.' *Even if it's only to say goodbye.*

'I can't. I gave my word.'

Defeated, she closed her eyes and nodded. Scott would never betray a confidence. She had no choice but to accept it.

'Give him the time he needs, Cleo. He'll be back when he's ready.'

'Will he?' Why hadn't he let her in? Even in his pain he'd held her at arm's length. Heart cramping, she gazed beyond the window, watching a jet's lights wink high in the sky. Perhaps because his heart now lay an ocean away on another continent. She thought of the café date he'd arranged. Or he'd found someone closer. She struck her palm against her thigh. 'I feel so powerless.'

'You love him.'

She continued to gaze out the window. 'I've waited for Jack more than half my life. Waited to grow up, waited for him to look my way, waited for him to come back. It's no secret to anyone but Jack.'

'Tough, isn't it? The waiting. The wanting.'

Cleo turned at the subtle undertone. Scott was hunched forward, forearms on his knees, his eyes unusually intense…and focused on her.

Uh-oh. *Scott?* How had she missed this? But he looked away, down at his hands. He made two fists, rubbed them together. 'You looked, and maybe you missed seeing Jack's response for a few years back then, but he was looking back.'

She felt those words all the way to her soul.

A corner of his mouth kicked up in a semi-grin as he finished, 'Discreetly, mind you.'

'Scott, I…' She mentally closed her eyes remembering Jack's first night back when she'd tried to kiss Scott to prove Jack didn't mean anything to her. *Stupid, stupid.* 'You're the big brother I never had. Something Jack could never be, because of how I felt about him.' How she'd always feel about him.

And not once in those six years had Scott made a pass at her. He'd never tried to be more than her perfect Sir Galahad.

Why not?

Somewhere in her brain a light switched on. Scott wasn't talking about waiting for her, about wanting her… A mix of disturbing emotions knifed through her. A strange heat danced through her belly. 'You… wanted…Jack.'

Their eyes met with new awareness and he nodded. 'Jack never knew, and I wasn't ready to deal with my own sexuality. I spent the past few years in denial. Then five months ago I met Jason.'

'Jason. Oh, Scott.' She knelt before him and grasped his hands still clenched on his thighs. 'Does Jeanne know?'

When he didn't reply, she tightened her hold. 'These days it's no big deal, and I know Jeanne will accept you and...Jason.'

He nodded, blew out a breath. 'Seems like now's a good time to bring it out in the open. You and I have both learned the painful lesson that secrets don't do us any favours.' His hands turned palms up and linked with hers. 'Enough for now, you've had a rough day. Jase'll be back soon and I'd rather not have him walk in on our conversation.'

'I'm sorry, but I don't want to go home, Scott. Those terrible secrets are embedded in that house. I don't think I can face them alone. At least not yet.' She laid her head on their joined hands.

'I invited you here, didn't I?' Dropping a kiss on her hair, he said, 'Take the main bedroom; it's got its own bathroom. You'll be more comfortable and it'll give you privacy. Jase and I'll take the spare room. Just give me a moment to grab our toiletries.'

She was too tired and wrung out to argue. 'Thanks.'

He tightened his grip on her hands briefly before releasing them and rose. 'Sleep in as long as you like. I'll see you tomorrow after work.'

* * *

That night Cleo lay in the dark, breathing the earthy, masculine scents of the room and listening to the muted TV on the other side of the wall.

Her world as she knew it had come apart. Her trust and her beliefs about family, life and love had been shattered. Her eyes had been opened and her innocent view of the world had altered for ever.

But Jack… Her heart squeezed tight, so tight she wondered that it didn't crumble. Jack's own beliefs had been shattered more violently, more personally, years ago.

No wonder he didn't trust family.

No wonder he wanted nothing to do with love.

Between spring-cleaning Scott's apartment to channel that nervous energy, checking job vacancies—because she'd need a job when she signed the house over to Jack—and talking Jeanne's ear off in the evening, Cleo should have been exhausted. But over the next couple of nights fragments of her life intruded on her dreams. Images of Jack's bruised body kept her awake and pacing the floor.

Somehow she had to show Jack that love and trust and family didn't have to be a lie. In her newly awakened view of the world, the one thing she could be sure of was her love for Jack. Everything else would grow from there.

That didn't mean she wasn't angry with him for keeping everything to himself. Before they sorted out their relationship one way or the other, she was going to set him straight—sharing was non-negotiable.

As dawn lightened the sky on the third day she took a shower and spent a long time letting the soothing spray massage her skin. Not bothering with a bra, she pulled on one of Scott's comfortable flannel shirts over her panties.

Creeping into the kitchen to make a hot drink, she noticed the microwave clock flashing five-thirty. She made a cup of chamomile tea and took it back to bed.

Slivers of pink and purple were streaking the sky when she stretched out and willed herself asleep.

As the aircraft dipped below the clouds on its final approach into Melbourne, Jack's gaze shifted from the early-morning glow to the small dog-eared photo in his hand. The man looking at the camera could have been him. Dark hair, olive skin, dimpled chin. Steve Jackson.

His father.

Regret churned through him for what he'd lost. But Steve Jackson had been killed before Jack had been born. His mother had named him for the man who'd given him life. She just hadn't bothered to inform Jack, or Gerry, as it turned out—he almost felt sorry for the man. Almost.

His mother had looked frail and weather-beaten from years out in the field, so he hadn't told her about the abuse that had begun after she'd left. His fingers tightened on the photo. Seeing her again had dredged up an inconvenient surge of emotion from some deep forgotten corner of his heart. Something of the same had reflected in her eyes as, out of some warped sense of duty, he'd kissed her goodbye.

He hadn't looked back.

She'd chosen her life, let her live it. It was time Jack Devlin chose his. A new determination coursed through him as he thought of Cleo. She'd probably still be asleep when he arrived, which would give him an opportunity to sneak in and wake her for once, instead of the other way round.

His blood pounded in anticipation as he thought about how he might accomplish that. His loins grew heavy just thinking of those long lashes fluttering open, her husky morning voice. That erotic feline way she'd arched her back and stretched as if waiting to be petted the last time they'd woken together.

But his heart tumbled over in his chest as he thought of the whole woman. A woman that got to him on every level. With every layer he'd peeled away, he'd discovered something new or long forgotten, from the creative way she stacked the unwashed dishes, to the soft core she guarded beneath all that attitude.

She could freeze him out with just one look and have him melting with another. She had drive and tenacity and, once she made up her mind, she let no one steer her off course. She also had compassion and empathy and put her needs on hold to help others—Gerry and himself for starters.

And he wanted it all, the complete package.

Family, Jack. But you wouldn't know about that. He looked at the photo in his hand again, before slipping it into his pocket. Perhaps he did now. He *did* know he was going to give it his best shot.

She'd been spitting mad when he'd left, understandably so. He'd been hurting too. Cleo had always been feisty and up front—another aspect that he loved about her. Scotty understood her too. His buddy would reassure her.

She knew how he felt about her. Hadn't they made mad, glorious love only hours before? She'd know he was coming back; he'd told her. He'd kept it low-key because of possible complications, but she didn't know any of that. Like any woman, she'd overreacted.

She'd wait. She'd told him she loved him. Rather, she'd spat it at him. A smile touched his lips and he let his head fall back on the headrest and closed his eyes. His whole body brimmed with something close to awe. Everything would be fine when he explained.

Rubber hit the tarmac with a thud and the aircraft roared as it slowed, then taxied, the low sun glinting bronze on the glassed terminal building as they neared.

A frustratingly slow hour later he paid off the cabbie and stared at her bedroom windows. One was open as usual, but the curtains were closed. Yes, still asleep.

He could almost believe he was nervous. He'd detoured to a florist for a peace-offering, and the scent of the long-stemmed carnations mingled with the familiar scent of morning-damp grass. Magpies warbled in the eucalypts. He had to force himself not to sprint to the front door.

This homecoming was so different from the one he'd faced a few weeks earlier. He wasn't coming home to a house. He was coming home to a woman. To family—his family. The warmth of that rightness seeped through his blood like the early-morning sunshine and settled comfortably in his bones.

A freeze-frame of Cleo, round with his baby, stopped him in his tracks. *Their* baby. He let out a breath. *Whoa. Back up. One step at a time.* Apologies and explanations first.

Letting himself in, he dumped his bag in the hall. He noticed it immediately. The stillness, the emptiness. No Con, no inviting breakfast smells.

Quick as spit, his buoyant mood evaporated. This didn't feel good. *I won't wait for you again.*

His heart lurching, he took the stairs two at a time. The unslept-in bed confirmed it. His fist tightened around the flowers. She loved this house—she *owned* it, for God's sake.

So where the hell was she?

He all but leapt down the stairs, snaffled keys from the hook in the kitchen and headed for Gerry's Daimler, praying there was enough fuel. *Think.* Where would she go? He didn't have Jeanne's phone number handy, but he keyed in Scott's mobile number. Voice mail. He swore, left a message and tossed the phone onto the seat.

Tyres screeching, he swung out of the drive and headed for Scott's apartment five minutes away. Jeanne would already be at the salon—Scott's place was closer. He saw Scott's flatmate Jason's car pull out as he turned into the apartment building's parking lot.

He leaned on the doorbell, tried the door. Finding it unlocked, he shoved it open and followed the smells of burnt toast and sounds of activity to the kitchen.

'Jack.' Scott was wiping what looked like the remains of cat food off the floor but he tossed the cloth on the sink when he saw him. 'I expected you to call—'

'I did; you didn't pick up. Where's…'

Scott's bedroom door opened off the L-shaped entertaining area and a sleepy-eyed woman stumbled out. In a too-big flannel shirt, and nothing much else by the looks of it. '…Cleo?'

He took in her quick indrawn breath, the wide, stunned eyes. 'Jack!'

His fleeting relief turned to something hot and sharp that slashed through him like a knife. He kept his eyes pinned to hers. He wanted to read the truth in those eyes. More, he wanted to avoid the bare legs and the ample show of cleavage that told a story he didn't want to hear.

A story that told him she didn't love him enough to wait. That she'd carried out her threat. That she'd turned to Scott, his mate. The stab of the twin-pronged betrayal had him itching to pound…something. Anything. Instead, he tightened his fist around the flowers, and, still watching her, he planted them firmly, squarely, on the coffee-table. 'Surprise.'

For a moment she seemed confused at the venom in his voice, which he hadn't tried to disguise. Then she glanced down at herself, one hand rising to fumble with the single closed button. 'I was…asleep…I…'

That husky morning voice that always turned him on scraped over his already raw emotions. Jack took a step back, still unable to comprehend the scene that was playing out right in front of him, like something from a soap opera. He glared at Scott, then Cleo, back to Scott again. 'What the *hell* is going on here?'

Scott moved to the table, stuffed some papers in his briefcase. 'You're jumping to the wrong conclusions, Jack.'

Jack's glare swung to the sofa. No evidence that anyone had spent the night on it. 'Am I?' The fact that Cleo stood between them prevented Jack from crossing the room and doing something he'd possibly regret later—or would he? 'Only one other bed... You telling me you're gay now, Scotty?'

Jack's ex best buddy exchanged a covert glance with Cleo as he snapped his briefcase shut. 'I'm due in court in an hour,' he said. 'I'll leave you to it.' He paused at the door. 'Tell him the truth, Cleo. All of it.'

And the door closed with a click.

The truth. How far back did that *truth* go? A chill settled over Jack's body like a shroud, almost suffocating him. Double-crossed by the two people he'd trusted above all others, who meant more to him than anyone.

He'd learned the rules young. Putting your heart out there on the landscape that was life was asking for it to be trampled on. Which was why he preferred the role of spectator, viewing life through the lens of his camera. Detached, alone, heart intact.

He hadn't learned a bloody thing.

'The truth then, Cleo,' he said at last, hearing the bleak sound of his own voice. Or perhaps it was the sound of his heart being torn apart. Irrevocably, finally.

She moved to the window. Avoiding eye contact. Avoiding him. The sun carved bars of gold over her through the vertical drapes, making her seem even more inaccessible.

'The *truth* is I couldn't stay at the house alone, Jack. Not after…' She seemed to shrink before his eyes, hugging her arms around herself. '…Scott told me about…your father.'

Great. Just great. He rubbed the back of his neck where a tension headache was beginning to throb. 'Let it go; I have.' She'd loved the man; Jack had wanted to spare her the gory details.

'What he did to you…' At last she turned to face him. A well of emotions darkened the misty blue of her eyes. 'I'm sorry—'

'I don't want your pity—'

'You don't have it,' she shot back. Gripping her upper arms with white-knuckled fingers, she glared at him. 'I was going to say I'm sorry you didn't tell me. What I *am* is *angry*. Why didn't you ever fight back? I never saw *him* bruised and battered.'

He shook his head. 'Fists, violence of any kind never solved anything. It frustrated the hell out of him when I didn't retaliate. The anger and unhappiness in his eyes each time I walked away gave me a twisted sense of satisfaction.'

'And didn't you think I had a right to know? All that time you let me love that man…'

'He loved you too.' The bastard. 'I didn't want to hurt you.'

'You kept the truth from me. You lied to me. You went away without a word and kept it to yourself. *That* hurts.'

'I—'

'Six years of your life are a mystery to me.' She

sliced her hand through the air, rattling the blinds and cutting him off. 'You never trusted me enough to open yourself to me, to let me in on your thoughts and experiences. *That* hurts. You're like the silver bangles I make. Beautiful, strong, solitary and *closed*.'

She shut her eyes, but a single tear tracked down one pale cheek. Jack yearned to pull her into his arms. He wanted her body against his. He wanted to catch that tear with his tongue and taste the saltiness, to share his own pain, a pain that right now was tearing his heart to shreds.

Yes, he'd hidden the truth about Gerry. And he'd do it again. But he'd kept too much from her. Gerry was one thing; shutting her off from the past six years was as bad as cheating. Letting her believe he'd been living a life of indulgence and women had been a ploy to keep her at arm's length, but it was still lying.

He'd been an idiot. If she'd turned to Scott for more than comfort, he had no one to blame but Jack Devlin. He'd deal with Scott later; right now he had to get Cleo back. He had to convince her that they belonged together. But not here. 'Get your stuff; we're going home.'

Her damp eyelashes flicked up and she looked at him, her eyes twin pools of blue misery. 'You can still call it home?'

'It's all we've got at the moment. Sometimes, Goldilocks, you have to face problems where they lie.'

Cleo stared at him. His voice was steel, his eyes like flint. But the message in his words… *We're going home.* The way he'd coupled them together sent hope soaring through her heart. If only. She wanted to believe. She dared not hope. Not yet.

'My car, Con…'

'I'll deal with Con. Get dressed; we'll pick up your car later.'

She cringed at the way his eyes slid over Scott's shirt. 'I didn't…' she began, but he'd already turned away to hunt up the cat.

Five taut, silent minutes later she sat in Gerry's car, staring at the house that had been given to her. Her mouth turned dust-dry, her body tightened a little more with every painful beat of her heart. Once upon a time she'd never imagined not belonging here.

Now she didn't belong anywhere. To anyone.

Jack sat beside her, his familiar scent surrounding her. She understood his wanting to go back to Rome. He'd made a new life there. At least her head understood, even if her heart couldn't accept it. Now she was independent it made sense he'd want to get on with the rest of his life without those bad memories.

She was part of those bad memories.

On legs that barely held her, she climbed out of the car, opened the carry cage and let Con out. He scurried away, then glared at her from beneath his favourite bush. 'Sorry, big guy,' she murmured. At least someone wanted to be here.

Turning, she saw Jack watching her from the driver's side, looking remote behind his sunglasses. 'Let's go,' he said. Curt and unsmiling. So not the way she'd imagined.

The moment Jack unlocked the door she fled

upstairs to her bathroom, closed the door. Grabbing her toothbrush, she cleaned her teeth to chase away the sour taste of dread and to regain some sense of normalcy.

An impatient knock on the door was accompanied by, 'If you're not out in one minute I'm coming in to get you.'

His ultimatum sent a tingle dancing down her spine. She rinsed, patted her mouth dry, and, bracing herself, opened the door.

But what she saw stopped her dead. Jack Devlin, stubble-jawed and totally masculine in tight blue jeans and white T-shirt, lying on her bed and surrounded by pink satin and lace.

But it was his eyes that held her. It was as if they could reach deep down and see into her soul. He held her heart and her will in those dark eyes.

As if tugged by their magnetism, she drifted across the room, stopping in the centre of her pink sheepskin rug. The faintest of breezes carried the delicate fragrance of morning, and Jack.

The muscles in his forearm twisted like rope as he plumped a frilly lace cushion and set it behind his head. 'We're going to talk; we might as well be comfortable.'

Talk. Honestly, she was all talked out. What she wanted was body contact and lots of it.

When she didn't answer, a corner of his mouth kicked up. 'Isn't that what you women want to do? Talk? Lay it all out on the table? Dissect and analyse and rehash?'

The sight of those more-than-capable hands and long, sensuous fingers as they smoothed the quilt beside him sent a thrill of remembrance racing to her feminine centre. 'At this particular moment, not especially. Is that what *you* want to do?'

The flash of heat in his eyes disappeared beneath a darker, sombre patina, lightning behind storm clouds. 'It's a start.' He jerked a thumb at the bed. 'Sit down. I've made up my mind about what I want to say and I'd rather say it with you beside me.'

She walked the rest of the way but perched herself on the edge of the rose-printed quilt and folded her hands. Took a deep breath. Swallowed. 'I'm listening.'

He rubbed at the back of his neck. 'I've been to see my half of the Dastardly Duo.'

She blinked in surprise. At no stage had either of them considered tracing the whereabouts of their respective absent parents. 'Why?'

'Take a look at this and tell me what you think.' He handed her a creased photo, warm from his pocket.

She saw a handsome dark-haired man with a dimple in his chin. 'He's the image of you,' she said slowly, comparing Jack and the photo. 'A relative?'

'He was my biological father. He's been dead for over twenty-seven years.'

Shock, disbelief and the chilling knowledge that they'd both been betrayed shivered through her. 'Gerry…Gerry's not your father.' Each word was wrung out of her.

'No. Gerry left some…info; I had to check it out.'

The cold, flat tone, the hard, obsidian eyes were a

Jack Cleo had never seen before. 'What information? Jack, you're scaring me.'

'Which is precisely why I couldn't tell you. Scared the hell out of me too. He told me mum had known your dad around the time I was born. A lie, but I had to be sure.'

She took a moment to absorb the implications. 'He thought my father was...yours too?' Her chest was too tight, her throat so dry she could barely get the words out.

'He *didn't* think it.' Jack's jaw tightened. 'Gerry just enjoyed messing with my head. Punishing me for learning he was sterile and the kid he'd raised all those years wasn't his own.'

'Oh, Jack.' That sense of betrayal erupted into an icy ball that left no room for the place in her heart where Gerry had been.

'There's more.' He put the photo on Cleo's night-stand before he continued. 'I haven't been fair to you. One of the reasons I haven't talked about those missing years is because some of it's not pretty.'

'It's okay,' Cleo urged, shifting closer. 'I want to know. All of it.'

He scrubbed a hand over his face. 'I landed a job as a fashion photographer in Rome for the first two years. After that I took up a post in the Middle East. I've seen first-hand what war does to families, children, lives. It affected me so much I stayed on to help.'

She frowned. 'Scott told me you were in Rome when he contacted you.'

He nodded. 'I was in hospital when I got the call.'

The gunshot wound.

He'd been in a *war zone*. She could sense it all: the desert haze, the terrible sounds of gunfire and men, the hot smell of metal and sweat, the cold shroud of fear. For a terrifying moment she was with him in that dark place looking into the jaws of hell.

Too agitated to sit still, she jumped up, paced away. She'd all but accused him of being with a woman when she'd seen that wound, and he hadn't said a word in his defence. She wanted to kick that stubborn, sexy backside into next week.

She swung to face him, a brew of anger and pride, admiration—and love—simmering in her heart. 'Silly stubborn…*man*. You put yourself in danger and I—'

Shrugging deprecatingly, he said, 'You'd prefer I walk away and pretend I didn't see?'

She almost laughed at the irony. 'Didn't you do exactly that to me, to us?' She was coming apart, but she pushed the words out over the lump in her throat. 'Is that what you're going to do now, Jack?'

He shook his head, watching her with a sensual heat that seemed to flow out to her like a deep-moving river. 'What I'm going to do now is something I've wanted to do for a very long time.'

CHAPTER TWELVE

CLEO didn't need the words to know what he wanted. What he intended. He was going to make love to her. The slow, bone-melting kind that she'd waited half a life time to share with him.

So why did she want to cry? Because that kind of loving came from the heart. At least it did in her books. It came with love and commitment.

Jack didn't believe in love and commitment.

Cleo believed in love. Despite her childhood, she believed in commitment. She longed to show Jack how love could mend the hurts of the past. She ached to unlock that something he'd closed off from the rest of the world. To give him a reason to stay.

To tell him she loved him without anger to taint the words.

And to hear those same words from his lips. She felt her eyes fill and blinked the moisture away.

His languid expression faded and his brows puckered. 'You have a problem with that?'

Definitely, absolutely. *It will hurt too much when you*

go. She swallowed over the ball of pain lodged tight in her throat and blurted, 'You're so clever, you figure it out.'

He stared at her, a help-me-out-here plea in his eyes. 'I can't think of a damn thing,' he said. 'Unless I was mistaken the other night…'

She remained where she was, too far away to touch him, but close enough to smell warm skin, to see the wear-and-tear marks on his medallion and the tiny gold flecks in his dark irises. 'The night we made love, I thought…' *You loved me.* She shook her head. Naïve and wishful dreams. 'I didn't think, neither of us did.'

'It doesn't always pay to think too hard,' he said softly, reaching for her.

And wasn't that the cold, hard truth? She stepped further out of his reach and said, 'I don't know how to play this. Relationships aren't my forte.'

With a rasp of denim over cotton quilt, he shifted on the bed so that his body angled towards her. 'You could start by coming over here.'

She hesitated, torn between throwing herself into his arms and running from the room. Neither option would give her what she craved.

'Come here, Goldilocks.' His tone dared her. 'Or are you afraid?'

'Oh, you don't play fair, Jack.'

'Cleo.' His eyes held a quiet torment. 'You've healed me, hit me, seduced me, refused me. And now you're damn near killing me.'

It wasn't a challenge or a dare. It was a simple plea that squeezed at her heart. Cautiously, she sat on the edge of the bed again. She didn't want to fool herself into thinking this was any different for him than any other woman he'd had. But, oh, if she could only convince him… 'Our relationship's always been a roller coaster ride.'

'But what a ride.' He sat up. She could feel the heat pumping from his body, his warm breath caressing her cheek as he spoke. 'And you're finally ready to admit we have a relationship. So am I,' he finished quietly.

His fingertip touched her nape. Barely there, but, oh, what a feeling. 'We practically grew up together,' she managed. 'Of course we have a relationship.'

'A very close, very personal, very intimate relationship.'

His finger slowly tracked down her spine, setting each vertebra on fire and making her shiver at the same time. Her eyes closed at the scorching, sensual pleasure. But she shook her head. 'You denied us that, Jack, when you left.'

'I'm not denying it now,' he muttered, his voice rough with emotion. 'Say yes, Goldilocks. Tell me you want me.'

Her body was melting like metal beneath her blowtorch. Her brain wasn't faring any better because she couldn't seem to remember why she'd thought letting the man she loved touch her was such a bad idea. She sagged against the solid wall of muscle behind her. 'Yes. Yes, Jack. I want you.'

With a low growl that vibrated against her back, he pressed his lips to the pulse in the sensitive hollow above her collar-bone. She felt her legs tremble as he tugged her gently to her feet with him so his thighs touched the backs of hers and his hands warmed her belly through her vest-top. So he surrounded her.

'I want to do things to you. I want my name on your lips when you come,' he murmured, and stroked a moist tongue over her ear lobe.

His words slid like mulled wine through her system, intoxicating her with their promise, blinding her to consequences. Jack wanted *her*, so-not-sophisticated Cleo Honeywell in her oldest vest-top and frayed jersey shorts.

The hot press of his palms on the soft cotton shifted lower. She felt the roughness of callused skin as his fingertips slid over her belly, the gentle glide of fabric as he eased shorts and panties down over her hips until they fell softly to her ankles.

Desire coiled low in her belly, dampening the place between her legs and filling her with restless anticipation. 'Jack…' Her arms seemed heavy as she lifted them, pushing her fingers through her short cap of hair, then twining them about his neck behind her so that her breasts lifted, tingling and full.

But he didn't touch them, not yet. He slid his hands over the cloth one more time, tracing the dip in her navel with a fingertip, then shimmied her top over her head. Her breasts spilled free, swollen and heavy.

'No bra,' he murmured.

'Was in a hurry.' Her pulse thundering in her ears, she waited on a razor's edge. She heard the rustle of fabric behind her as he stripped off his own clothes.

At last he turned her in his arms. His gaze locked

with hers. She saw his need in the dark soulful eyes, felt it in the quivering muscles in his arms. Felt that need nudge hot and hard against her belly.

It made her feel female and powerful.

He disabused her of that notion when he swept her up and laid her on the bed as if she weighed no more than a puff of air. He was the one in control here—but he was the one trembling.

A rainbow danced overhead as the sun-catcher in her window twisted in the breeze, catching the glints of chestnut in his hair. For a long hot moment they simply stared at each other. She absorbed the long, lean lines of him, from the broad, muscled shoulders, to the tapered waist, to the brutally masculine jut of his sex.

He drew in a long, unsteady breath. 'You have the most exquisitely beautiful body I've ever seen.'

And for the first time in her life she felt beautiful. Almost as beautiful as the models he worked with. But perhaps he was a mind-reader because he said, 'I want to photograph you, just as you are now.'

'Really?' She shifted on the cool coverlet, restless with the promise in his husky voice, aching with need under his scorching, sensuous gaze.

'Really.' Sinking to the bed, he stretched out over her, his spread knees capturing her hips. He held her face in his hands as if he held something special. 'Later,' he whispered, and lowered his mouth.

Surprisingly soft. Sinfully seductive. He was all she could think of—his unique taste, the scrape of stubble against her chin, the caress of his breath on her cheek.

Hot, masculine flesh rubbed against her belly, one hard-packed muscled thigh between hers. She heard her own low moan as she clutched the hard curve of a shoulder, rubbing her aching nipples against the plush roughness of his chest.

Sensing her need, he eased her back. 'Let me.' He filled a hand with her breast, rubbed a maddeningly slow thumb over the tip. 'So firm, so beautiful.'

'So oversized,' she whispered, hearing the trace of her earlier vulnerability creep into her voice.

'Never.' He cupped both breasts in his palms. 'See? The perfect fit.'

He lowered his head again. The deep, wet pull of his mouth on her nipple, the slow, gentle glide of his hand over her belly, her hip. He suckled the other breast while his fingers parted her woman's flesh, slipped a finger inside her and slid it out slowly. Over and over. His unhurried gentleness, the fine tremor in his hands undid her.

And frustrated her. Somewhere in her befuddled senses, she was aware of the tension behind the quiver, the strain in his breathing. He was holding back. 'Jack—'

He groaned. 'For once in your life don't argue with me.'

'But, Jack… Now,' she begged.

'Demanding woman,' he muttered against her ear. But she heard the smile settle in his voice as he pressed her into the mattress. 'I'm going to have to teach you to be patient. Especially in the bedroom.'

'Might take a lot of practice.' In the bright light of

morning, his two-day beard showed up stark and bristly against his tan, reminding her of what he'd been through the past two days.

He was here now, and she revelled in the hot, hard weight of him. Revelled in the feel of flesh sliding against slick flesh, the scent of morning and hot skin filling the musky air between them. Lifting her hips, gripping his arms, she opened to him, poised at the edge of her control, desperate for this completion, this merging of bodies, of selves.

Eyes locked on hers, he eased himself inside—slowly, drawing out the moment, filling her with his heat and strength. Her inner muscles quivered, drawing his hard, throbbing length inside her until she couldn't tell where she ended and he began.

He muttered something she didn't catch; cursing God or thanking Him. His eyes still focused on her, only her, he withdrew slowly before thrusting into her again, with more insistence.

The harsh groan torn from his throat sounded like music to her ears, her own rising to accompany him. Her heart beat against his in a duet of passion. He filled her, completed her.

His hands found hers, palm to palm, fingers entwining, then he dragged her down into the velvet depths of passion in those dark eyes only to toss her up to a place full of light and life. And love.

Sensation pin-wheeled over sensation, creating a whirling galaxy of jewels, each one glittering and unique. She caught the edge of the spiral as it hurtled towards the stars, higher and higher. She wished it could go on and on, that she could gather all those precious treasures to her heart and hold them for ever.

But Jack wasn't a for ever guy.

So she had now, and the little dip in her happiness smoothed out as he pinned her hands with his above her head. Breath mingled. Sweat slicked their bodies. There wasn't an inch of skin that wasn't melded with his.

Then he thrust hard once, twice, and liquid warmth flooded inside her as he shuddered, rasping out her name and taking her to the stars with him.

Cleo floated back to earth. To reality. To the soul-destroying knowledge that Jack still had a job overseas, a life beyond Melbourne suburbia. Right now he was sprawled half on, half off her, in no apparent rush to change the status quo.

She closed her eyes, reliving their lovemaking, storing it for later. But wait… Had he said, *I'm going to have to teach you to be patient*? A glimmer of hope lit inside her. Did that mean he wanted to stay a little longer? With her?

As if he'd heard her thoughts, she felt Jack push up. When she opened her eyes his head was propped on one elbow and he was watching her. Serious eyes. Serious mouth. No more body contact.

'Cleo—'

Shaking her head, she sat up, wishing she had the sheet to cover her. 'Don't.' *Don't spoil what we shared, don't take that away from me.*

He captured her wrist. 'Listen to me. I need you, Cleo, and not only in bed. My life's a dull black and white without you.'

What? What was he telling her? 'Say that again,' she said slowly.

'You colour my world, Goldilocks.' He sat up too, and cupped her face. 'You have looks, loyalty, courage and optimism. You're the most beautiful person I've ever known, inside and out.'

She wished she didn't hear a *but* coming. For the sake of her pride, for her heart, she forced a smile. 'That's the best recommendation I ever had.'

He frowned and she could see he was offended. 'I'm being serious here, I'd appreciate it if you'd be too.'

'Okay. On a serious note, then...' She dug down deep for some of that courage to say, 'I overheard you making a date at Café Medici the other day. You laughed—the way you always laugh when it's a woman on the phone.' She ignored his raised brows. 'You told *whoever* you were interested. When you didn't tell me about it, I assumed...' She lifted a shoulder. 'So, what are you trying to tell me here, Jack? Because I sure as heck don't follow.'

He looked thoughtful a moment, then he grinned. 'You reneged on our shower. I was discussing a job opening for a photo-journalist. In Australia.'

Australia. That glimmer of hope flared, but she had to know more before she started tap-dancing. 'Why would you do that? What about your other...interests?' She studied his face, searching for subtle cues as she said, '*Ciao, bella* ring any bells?'

Another brief pause. 'Carmela,' he said finally. 'She and her husband Domenic rented me a room when I first landed the job in Italy. Domenic's ill. Carmela's been updating me on his progress.'

'Not Liana.' Had she really said that aloud? Oops. Big mistake bringing up a past lover.

'Liana…? Ah, the Armenian designer. Haven't seen her in years.' He narrowed his eyes. 'And you know her how…?'

'Um, a magazine…?'

'Milan.' His eyes lit with gentle teasing. 'Does that mean you were jealous?'

I've been hung up on a woman he hasn't seen in years. She swiped at his shoulder. 'What do you think? I love you, Jack, that's unconditional. It's not a choice, it simply is. Doesn't mean I didn't hate you for leaving me. Twice.' She prodded his chest. 'And for not telling me about the job opening in Australia.'

'That was an hour before I read Gerry's letter. You were in a snit at breakfast, didn't seem like the time to—'

'Because of the phone call,' she interrupted, prodding him again, harder.

'I didn't know that, now, did I? I wanted to tell you over a celebration dinner. I wanted to tell you…' His tone turned sombre as he trailed off, rubbing the back of his neck. Nervous. Definitely nervous.

'Hey,' she said softly, and tugged his arm, felt the ropey sinews twist beneath her palm. 'Tell me now. We're both naked here, seems like a good time to bare our thoughts as well.'

He nodded, fingering a spike of her hair and kissing her forehead. 'I've learned from you these past weeks.

Your commitment to family and your inner strength gave me the courage to look inside myself. I discovered something greater than my fear. Love.'

A lump rose in her throat. She looked into those eyes that knew her so well. Not vulnerable and guarded now, but clear and filled with hope. She pressed her palm to the side of the face she loved. 'I'm glad I could help.'

He covered her hand with one of his. 'Only you.'

'So, you're ready to come home.'

'I want to spend the rest of my life with you; it doesn't matter where. You *are* my home.'

His lips found hers, letting all the emotion of his words flow into one long, deep kiss. Then he lifted his head just enough to look into her eyes and say, 'I love you, Goldilocks; I always have.'

Her heart wept for joy. Words more precious than diamonds. 'Can I have that in writing?' she murmured against his mouth.

'You bet.'

Wrapping her arms around his neck, she pressed herself against him, mouth to mouth, skin to skin, heart to heart. She felt his hands, hard, possessive, seeking, as they slipped around her waist, over her back, circled over her shoulders and finally, finally found her aching breasts.

He leaned back to look at what he was touching, and a hot tide of lust and love washed through her. No one had ever been able to turn the heat up like Jack. 'You've made me feel good about myself,' she whispered. 'You even make me feel sexy and desirable.'

'Even?' He shook his head. 'Get this through that beautiful, stubborn head, Cleo. You *are* sexy and desirable. And much, much more. It's not your clothes or the way you wear your hair. It's *you*.' He leaned back to look into her eyes. 'Marry me, Cleo. Let me spend the rest of my life showing you.'

The sexy rumble of his voice echoed deep in her heart, filling all those empty places only Jack could fill. Tears sprang to her eyes. 'Oh, Jack, yes. Yes, I'll marry you. But I don't want to wait.' She pulled his long, hot and incredibly sexy body on top of her. 'Start showing me now.'

A long time later, their bodies warm, sated and entwined, Cleo twirled Jack's well-worn medallion in her fingers. 'You never forgot your roots, did you? After all that happened, even when you were injured, you cared enough to come back.'

'To you, Goldilocks.' He pressed an open-mouthed kiss against her neck.

She basked in the stunning sensation, her happiness spilling over when he murmured, 'Is a month enough time to organise a wedding?'

'As long as I can find a dress to knock your socks off. And lingerie, and sleepwear…' If she needed sleepwear. Her mind spun at the images.

'Speaking of sexy outfits,' he said, in sync with her thoughts, 'do you still have that black catsuit around here somewhere? I'd like another chance to take it off you.'

Arching her foot over his leg, she slid it down his shin, enjoying her new-found role of seductress as his body jerked to attention. 'I think that can be arranged.'

EPILOGUE

JACK waited for his wife to finish duty-free shopping with Jeanne at Melbourne International. Cleo had refused to let him accompany her, saying she couldn't shop with him breathing down her neck. He planned to do a lot of that. Tonight.

His wife. He tried unsuccessfully to wipe the silly grin off his face that seemed to have become a habit over the past few weeks. They'd been married in a small civil ceremony less than five hours ago. He still couldn't quite believe it.

They'd put the house up for sale and were going to tour Italy and catch up with Domenic and Carmela before settling in Melbourne's suburbs. The clichéd white picket fence was looming closer.

He didn't mind a bit.

He turned to his best man. 'Scotty, you and Jason have a major responsibility there looking after Constantine.' He was still getting used to seeing Scott and his partner as a couple, but he'd never seen his buddy so relaxed.

'Don't worry about the big guy,' Scotty said. 'He'll be fine until you get back. Your bride's on her way,' he said with a grin, glancing over Jack's shoulder.

Jack turned. And there she was, all lusciously curved five-feet two of her in crisp white slacks and an emerald jacket, confetti still stuck to her spiked hair, eyes sparking with excitement, her face aglow.

He didn't need his camera to know he'd remember the scene for ever—and the one of her in her spectacular dress as they exchanged vows. But he snapped a shot anyway before saying, 'Hi.'

She answered with a breathless 'hi' of her own. That husky sigh got to him every time, on every level. He stepped closer, relieving her of a mountain of shopping bags. Their gazes fused, their hands brushed. The air between them flared with heat.

They were in the middle of a noisy tide of humanity, lights and announcements, but all he could focus on was the subtle scent of her skin and the way her lips curved as she shared the moment with him.

Somewhere to his left, he heard Jeanne cough loudly, then say, 'Come on, you two. Get on board that aircraft before we all start melting here.'

'We're on our way.' With his eyes still on Cleo's, he raised her left hand, pressed a kiss to the gold-set ruby flanked by diamonds and the filigree wedding band Cleo had made herself. His own matching band glinted in the airport lights. 'Ready?' he said.

She nodded, her blue eyes as warm as the summer sky. 'Oh, yes, I'm ready.' Her smile widened. 'I've been ready for a very long time.'

Their eyes lingered a second or two over their joined fingers. He smiled back, filled with love for the woman who was his wife. 'Then let's get started.'